DISCONNECT

IRON BULLS MC #2

PHOENYX SLAUGHTER

COPYRIGHT

DISCONNECT (IRON BULLS MC #2)

Disconnect (Iron Bulls MC #2)

Edited by: Hot Tree Editing
Digital ISBN: 978-1-943950-90-4
Print ISBN: 978-1-943950-82-9

In the second book in the thrilling Iron Bulls Motorcycle Club series, shocking secrets are exposed. Lives are forever changed.

Who's telling the truth? Who's lying?

Who can Karina Trust?

Can the passionate bond of two screwed-up people survive the whirlwind trying to tear them apart?

ALSO BY PHOENYX SLAUGHTER

Asunder (Iron Bulls MC #1)

Disconnect (Iron Bulls MC #2)

Entwined (Iron Bulls MC #3)

Vexed (Iron Bulls MC #4)

Unhinged (Iron Bulls MC #5)

Dirty Side Down (Iron Bulls MC Boxed Set #1)

Infatuation

CHAPTER ONE

DANTE

How could I let this happen?

Luck and I have been driving Interstate 10 lookin' for any sign of Karina for hours.

My job, my role in the club revolves around protecting what's important.

Yet, I failed my girl. And somehow over the last few weeks, she's become the most important thing to me.

Don't know where the fuck she is. Don't know why the fuck Hemi kidnapped her.

Well, I can guess why.

He has a death wish.

We tore through the rest stop Karina called me from. No sign of her. Janitor said he remembered seeing her with some guy. They left maybe ninety minutes ago.

Ninety minutes.

"You want to give Romeo an update?" Luck asks. My mind's a fuckin' mess so Luck's behind the wheel. Took his SUV since there's a good chance we'll be carting Hemi's dead fuckin' body home.

"Tell me about her."

Great, Luck thinks I'm so fucked in the head he's trying to get me talkin'.

I must be fucked up, because I answer.

"Somehow we just fit together."

"How'd she end up living with you?"

My shoulders jerk and I stare out the window. "I didn't like where she was living."

"So you moved her into your cabin?"

"She needed someone to look after her." Too bad, I fucked it up.

"You ever had a sub before?"

"No. I ain't got time for all that crazy shit you're into."

Luck snorts at that. "Lazy prick."

We fall silent again and I keep watching the scenery. "She calls me Daddy."

"Ahh. Baby girl subs are the best kind."

"What?"

"Littles. Never mind. Just, treat her with care."

"I fuckin' try. Feel like I fucked up big now."

"This ain't on you. How the fuck could you know a brother would pull a stunt like this?"

"He's been up in our business since day one. Way he's been acting, I shoulda seen it comin'."

Karina

I'm so freaking scared. Logan's barely said a word to me since he tied me to this damn chair. He paced behind me for a long time, and then went outside to make a phone call. As much as I strained to listen, I only got bits and pieces of the conversation.

"He should be gone…it should be clear. They're gonna kill…so you better…"

None of it sounds good.

The slam of the door when he steps inside startles me.

"We need to talk."

Gathering my courage, I answer as calmly as I can. "You need to let me go, Logan."

"I can't go back after this. I want you to come with me."

He's already kidnapped me, what more does he want?

"I don't want to. I want to go home."

His face contorts into rage. "To Dante? That's not your home, Karina. He'll hand you off to one of the brothers when he's done with you.

"That's not true," I whisper.

"He's a fuckin' killer, Karina. He murders people for the club. That's his job."

My heart thuds. Prickles shiver over my skin. Not my Dante. "He takes care of me," I whisper.

"He's never hurt you? Would you even know the difference?"

"Fuck you! You have no right after what you did."

"Karina, believe me when I tell you I had a very good reason for what I did."

"Well, I got the message from your friend loud and clear."

Shock ripples over his face. His eyebrows draw down and he cocks his head to the side. "What the fuck you talkin' about?"

"Let me go."

As if being tied to the chair isn't leaving me defenseless enough. He's going to strip every last bit from me. His hands curl over my shoulders, shaking me until I look at him. "After you dumped me. The guy you sent to make sure the message stuck."

"Karina, I never sent anyone to see you."

He's lying. I know he is. Even as his hand brushes over my cheek in a tender gesture, I haven't felt from him in ages, I know it's a lie. "Honey, your dad threatened me. I needed time to get in with the club, make some money so I could get you out of his house, and put you through school—"

"Stop lying!"

He recoils, staggers back, and drops into the chair across from me. "I never stopped loving you, Karina. I just needed time."

"That's bullshit. My dad's never even home."

"I couldn't have you living with me at the clubhouse. You see what it's like there. I was saving up to get us a place."

"If that's true, why didn't you tell me?"

"I couldn't."

"Why have that guy come and do what he did to me—"

"What guy? Karina, I swear to God, I never." He stops and stares at me as my words sink in. "What did he do to you?"

I can't look at him. But I can't close my eyes either, or the image of the dark stranger forcing me—*no.*

CHAPTER TWO

DANTE

"YOU GOT some sort of tracking thing on her phone? You know, in case it gets lost or stolen?" Luck asks after a few more miles.

"I don't think so."

"Does she have email on it?"

Why the fuck didn't I think of that sooner? My brain isn't functioning. Any skills I've gotten through years with the club are turning to shit over this girl.

"You should be able to log into the device manager and track it that way if the phone's on."

"Yeah, after she called, what are the chances he kept the phone on him?"

Luck shrugs. "It's worth a try."

After going through a thousand screens and prompts, I'm ready to throw my phone out the window when Luck pulls over and snatches the phone out of my hands. "Signal's shitty out here," he mutters, as he's tapping in a bunch of shit. "Do you know her email?"

"No, but I installed a throw-away email on it to set the phone up. It should still be attached to it."

He puts in the information I give him and we wait.

And wait.

"The phone was on Interstate 10." That's good. It confirms what Karina told me before Hemi cut us off.

Luck taps and hums some more. "This..." he trails off and I'm ready to fuckin' throttle him. He tips up his head then glances back down at the phone.

"What?"

"Last hit was off exit 81."

"That's not that far up."

Luck hands me the phone and pulls back onto the highway.

"Here," he mutters as he guides us off the highway. A few miles down the road, there's a cheap motel. It's as good a place to start as any other. We circle the building, but there's no sign of Karina's car.

"He might have ditched it," Luck says, as if he's been reading my mind.

"Stop by the front office."

I whip out my phone and flip through my photos, looking for a non-sexy shot of Karina. I stumble over one she sent me earlier in the week. Said her friend Athena took it, so I wouldn't forget her while I was gone. I shake my head; she's standing in front of a row of lockers.

Christ, she's fucking *young*. What the fuck have I been doing—bringing her into my fucked up life?

Except she knew Hemi long before we met. Whatever this is, it isn't completely my fault.

I'm still furious.

Luck and I storm into the lobby. The clerk's eyebrows shoot up when he sees us. By the nervous twitch at the corner of his mouth, he knows what the Iron Bulls MC patch means.

Good, because I'm in no mood to fuck around.

"You seen this girl?" I ask, flashing him the picture of Karina.

"No, man. She your daughter?"

Motherfucker. "No," I snap.

Luck flashes what I guess is a picture of Hemi. Glad he came prepared because I don't have a picture of the walking corpse.

"What about him?"

"No. Sorry. You keep going that way"—he points north—"you'll run into a bunch of bigger chain motels. Keep going south; there's another cheap motel. It's back off the road a ways."

"Thanks."

We step outside. It's not even a question.

We're heading south.

Karina

"Karina, what guy?"

I can't. The tone of his voice. The remorseful look on his face. I'm starting to doubt everything I thought I knew.

"After we broke up. One night this guy woke me. Hurt me. Told me to stay away from you."

Logan's cheeks turn red and he scrubs his hand over his face. "Baby, I would never. No."

"I always assumed because of the way we broke up—"

"Do you know who it was?"

My eyes close and I'm right back in my bedroom. Suffocating while the stranger delivers his cruel message through whispers in my ear. "I never got a good look at him." His voice. His scent. I'll never forget those."

Logan's gaze darts to the door. "Please don't get mad—"

Harsh laughter bubbles out of me. "Mad? We passed mad a long time ago, Logan. You kidnapped me, and currently, have me tied to a chair. Or did you forget that?" I wiggle my hands at him. To remind him of what he's done, but also because they're starting to go numb.

He hesitates. "I can't let you go yet."

"Fine. Whatever you're about to say can't be worse than *kidnapping* me. I'm already furious with you."

Logan seems surprised. What, did he think I'd be on board with this nonsense?

"Your dad probably sent that guy."

My father? Kenneth Rivers is neglectful, sure. He's gone for long stretches of time for work. But to deliberately set me up to be…violated?

"Why?"

"To keep you away from me."

"Why? We've known each other forever."

"He was pissed I got involved with the club." His eyes close and he runs his hand over his hair. "Which is ridiculous since he's the one who introduced me to Romeo in the first place."

"Wait. What? My father introduced you to the MC? He doesn't know any bikers."

Logan levels a stern look at me. "Karina, I'm afraid you know fuck-all about your dad."

"Let me go, Logan."

"I can't, Karina. You'll go right back to him."

"To who? Dante. Of course I will."

Even though he already seemed to know this, his face contorts with anger. "What does Athena think of him?"

My head's spinning from the change in conversation. "What does she have to do with anything?"

"She's your best friend."

I shrug. "I don't know. She's just happy I'm finally over you."

My words are the slap in the face he needed. "I'm sorry I hurt you, Karina. I didn't know what else to do."

"Fine. You've had your say. My father scared you away. You weren't man enough to stand up to him and didn't have the balls to tell me. Thanks for clearing that up. Now, let me go."

"I can't let you go. Not until I make this right."

He sounds so sad, I almost believe him. But it doesn't matter now. "You can make it right by letting me go."

"There are things you don't understand. I don't know how—"

"I'm literally a captive audience, Logan. Whatever it is, spit it out! Nothing you say will hurt as much as what you're doing to me right now."

He hesitates. For a second I think he's finally come to his senses and will release me. Instead, he stands and paces, then stops to look at his phone. "Are you hungry?"

I am, but I'm too pissed to worry about food. "No."

"I'll run out and grab some food."

His hand closes over the doorknob. Is he kidding?

"Logan. You can't leave me here like this." Too late, I realize I shouldn't have shouted at him.

He glances back, forehead wrinkling, like he just realized my hands might be bound, but my mouth is free. Instead of releasing me, he grabs a hand towel from the bathroom.

"What are you doing?"

He twirls it into a rope.

"No. Logan. You can't. What if I choke or get sick or something happens to you while you're out? Or there's a fire? I could die. You can't leave me bound and gagged by myself." I'm babbling like crazy trying to get him to understand how stupid his plan is.

But he catches the towel in my mouth and ties it tight around my head. Then he walks out the door, locking it behind him.

Dante

The last clerk wasn't kidding. This place left cheap motel behind a few years ago. We circle the building but again there's no sign of Karina's car.

"Let's ask anyway," Luck says, as if it was even a question.

A young kid's behind the desk and he recognizes the picture of Hemi right away. "Yeah, I think so. He wasn't wearing no cut though when I saw him. Checked in couple hours ago."

I don't bother asking about Karina. Ain't gonna find her without Hemi. "What room?" I ask.

He shakes his head as if he's about to tell me he can't give out that information, then seems to decide it's not worth the beating we'll give him if he refuses.

Instead of words, he reaches behind him and grabs a key. I snatch it out of his hand and stomp out the door. Luck follows me to the room at the end of the building.

I knock twice. Except for the distant sound of traffic out on the main road, the area is quiet.

"Karina?"

This time a muffled scream comes through. Even distorted, I recognize my girl's voice. I can't work the key in the lock fast enough. Then I'm bursting in the door. My girl's tied to a fucking chair.

"Baby girl, I'm here." I pop the rag out of her mouth and start working on the ropes around her wrists. "Luck, help me."

Together, we get her free, and I run my hands over her wrists and ankles. She throws herself against me, sobbing so hard, I'm shaking with rage. "It's okay, baby girl, I got you."

Somewhere in the back of my head, I'm surprised at the soothing, nonsense sounds I'm using to calm Karina down.

"Where is he?"

She pulls back and shakes her head. Fury at the idea of her protecting him amplifies my anger. She seems to sense it and works to get the words out.

"Let me get her some water, Dante," Luck says, stepping outside. I'd forgotten all about him.

He brings a bottle in from the car. "It's warm," he says apologetically as he hands it to her.

She takes a couple sips, her eyes never leaving my face.

"I don't know," she finally gets out. "He said he was going to get food. I begged him not to leave me tied up. I was so scared something would happen and I'd be trapped…" the rest of her words are lost to harsh sobbing.

Behind me, Luck curses. "Jesus Christ, you never leave someone alone tied up. What the fuck?"

"No shit," I mutter.

Karina hiccups and takes another sip of water before setting the bottle down. She throws her arms around me, almost knocking me on my ass.

Turning my head, I meet Luck's concerned gaze and nod. "Give us a minute."

"Yeah. I'll wait in the truck in case he comes back; so he doesn't get spooked."

He shuts the door behind him.

I stand, lifting Karina into my arms. "Come 'ere." Gently, I settle us on the bed with my back to the headboard and her in my lap.

"Are you okay? Did he hurt you?"

She sucks in a few shaking breaths and sniffles. "No. But I was so scared."

We don't speak for a bit. The weight of her body comforts me. Fuck knows what I'm going to do about this. These *feelings* she's stirred up in me. I don't even care. Just want to take care of my girl.

CHAPTER THREE

KARINA

SOMEHOW, Dante found me. Relief and happiness overwhelm me. Also, fear, because I'm afraid of what Dante will do to Logan if he finds him.

I'm furious, but I don't want Logan dead.

I don't want Dante to be the one to kill him. I can't handle that.

"Tell me what happened, baby girl," he says after I calm down.

I sit up to organize my thoughts. Being pressed against Dante like this is making my body want inappropriate things.

Even though only a few hours have passed, it feels like months. I have to stop and think. "I ran out to the store to grab something. I was making you dinner."

The corners of his mouth turn up and he squeezes my hand.

"When I got back Logan was waiting. He said you sent him to pick me up because the club was on lockdown and he was taking me to meet you at the club's safe house."

He runs his hand through his hair, making it stick up in every direction. "Shit, baby girl. I shoulda explained things to you. Club's ever on lockdown, I'll bring you to the clubhouse. I'd never send Logan—"

"I didn't think so but I wasn't sure."

"I know. Not your fault. I'll tell you right now. If I can't be there, I'd send Luck," he nods at the door. "Whip's our RC, so if I can't get you, he'd be someone else I trust. Romeo, our president. He's a pig, but he wouldn't hurt you. But baby, I'd call you, something, so you knew what to expect."

"He said I wasn't important enough for you to worry about. That's why you sent him, and didn't call."

Dante pauses and glances away. "I know we haven't been together long, Karina. But you ain't some slampiece to me. I don't know of a single man in the club who wouldn't do everything possible to protect their ol' lady."

My nose wrinkles. Ol' lady? I prefer when he calls me his baby girl. He seems to sense it because he chuckles and runs the back of his hand over my cheek. "The women who're important to them," he explains.

"Oh." I'm so ashamed for letting Logan's words mess with me.

"What else, baby girl?"

I shrug because I'm not sure how to put into words the crazy shit that came out of Logan's mouth.

"He said you sent him to Mexico to get killed because of me."

Dante's face turns to stone. "Motherfuckin' pussy. That ain't true. It's a tough run, but all of us have done it."

I'm shocked because it's the most he's ever told me about club stuff.

"He said you kill for the club."

If it's possible, his face locks down even harder.

"I *protect* the club."

My fingers trace over his jaw. "I don't care. I just care that you're good to me. You've treated me better than anyone in my life. Logan was furious when I explained that to him."

Dante's jaw works, but he doesn't say anything.

"I don't deserve you," he finally mutters.

Dante

THERE'S NO EXCUSE.

None.

I know full well what kind of fucked up life I've chosen. Got no business bringing an innocent girl into it. Especially, if I ain't gonna keep her safe.

Club's had it easy the last few years. It's made me soft. Throw Karina into the mix and I'm a ball-less pile of mush. Been too busy worrying about sticking my dick in her, rather than explainin' shit to her.

"What else, baby girl?"

"Nothing, just a lot of nonsense."

I want more answers from her, but I think she's done. She yawns and I pull her against me, reassuring her that she's okay. Hell, reassuring myself.

A low knock interrupts our quiet. The door eases

open and Luck pokes his head in. His mouth turns up as he takes us in.

"A car drove through the lot, but didn't stop. Not sure if it was him and he made me or it was nothing."

I give him a description of Karina's car and he shakes his head. "Doesn't mean anything. He coulda dumped her car and gotten another," Luck says. I nod at him to come in and he shuts the door behind him.

"You okay, Karina?" he asks gently.

She nods, her cheek sliding over my chest and her arms tighten around my middle. Luck smiles as he takes a seat at the table.

"It's been over an hour, brother. What're you thinking?" he asks.

I glance down at Karina who seems to have fallen asleep. I don't know what the fuck to do.

I want to wrap both hands around Hemi's throat and stare into his eyes while I choke the life out of him. Since that doesn't seem to be an option, we should probably head home. No reason to keep my girl in this filthy motel any longer.

"Let's head back."

Luck nods. "Should probably keep her at the clubhouse until we figure this out."

My first instinct is to tell him to fuck off, don't tell me how to take care of my girl. Except, he's right. Even with all my degenerate, fucktard brothers around, she'll be safe there.

Leaning down, I press my lips to her forehead. Yeah, that's how far gone I am. Don't give a shit about my brother seein' me bein' all sweet with her. "Baby girl, wake up. We're gonna head back."

She shifts, snuggling into me tighter, and mumbles. Luck stands and chuckles.

"Can you take her?"

Alarm crosses his face for a brief second, but he scoops her out of my lap, holding her until I'm up and able to take her.

We get her settled in the back seat and get on the road. It's dark and I'm fighting exhaustion. When we're maybe halfway home, I twist to check that she's still asleep.

"If something happens to me, promise you'll look after her."

Luck's driving so he only glances at me for a second. "Why you thinkin' like that, brother?"

"Nothing. This whole fuckin' mess is making me realize I should make sure she's better taken care of. He told her I sent him to pick her up because the club was on lockdown and he was takin' her to our safe house."

"Don't be so hard on yourself. You haven't been together that long. She's young. It's not a stretch that you wouldn't have shared everything with her."

"No. But he used that against her. Someone else could too." I stare straight ahead. "I told her she can trust you. I'd send you. Explained we ain't got a safe house."

"Good."

"But beyond that. We all know the risks. You seem to understand...know her needs. So if something happens to me, I want *you* to make sure she's okay."

Luck doesn't seem to know what to say to that.

I think of how to explain it better. "I don't want someone like Romeo gettin' his hands on her."

"Yeah. I hear what you're saying. Of course. But can we not talk about something happening to you. It's bad luck."

I can't help laughing at that. "I ain't sayin' 'fuck my girlfriend,' bro. Just—"

"Yeah, I got it," he says with a snicker.

"I'd want you in my role too. But Romeo already knows that."

"Thanks."

Feelings time over, I relax into the seat and plan how I'm going to murder Hemi when I find his disloyal ass.

CHAPTER FOUR

KARINA

"Wake up, baby girl."

"Dante?"

My mouth's dry and my tummy's queasy. It's dark. I realize I'm in the back of an SUV, covered with a blanket. Blinking, I sit up. We're stopped.

The back door opens and I scramble backwards.

Dante pokes his head in and holds out his hand to me. I grab it gratefully and he tugs me out, wrapping me in his arms. "We're at the clubhouse. Gonna stay here for a bit until things calm down."

I'd rather be alone with him at the cabin. He seems to understand. His hand runs over my head and down my cheek. "It'll be safer for now."

This is the quietest I've ever seen the Iron Bulls clubhouse. Even the club girls are muted.

Romeo storms from one of the rooms and over to us. Gone is the wise-ass perv face I remember.

"You find him?" he barks at Dante.

"No."

Romeo lifts his chin at me. "She okay?"

Never mind me. I'm just standing right here.

"Yeah. I'm gonna keep her here for a day or two."

Romeo's gaze shifts to me, but none of the lewd comments I'm expecting come out. "You okay, sweetheart?"

I'm too shocked to answer with words, so I nod instead.

That's about all the civility Romeo's capable of. He raises an eyebrow at Dante. "When you're done reuniting, meet me in the chapel."

Dante's response is to wrap his arm around me tighter.

"You can fill me in while we're waitin' for him," Romeo says to Luck.

Without thinking about it, I reach for Luck's hand. "Thank you," I whisper. I feel terrible that it took me this long to say it.

Luck raises an eyebrow as if he's surprised. "You're welcome, Karina."

Dante walks me into the bathroom and strips me down. I sway on my feet and hold onto his shoulders for balance, making him smile.

He pulls me to him and strokes my hair. "I got you, baby girl."

My breath catches and I choke back a sob. No one has ever taken care of me or comforted me this way. I can't resist nuzzling against him. He shifts to open the shower stall door and flip the spray on. After waiting for the temperature to adjust, he nudges me inside.

"I'll be right back. Take your time."

I'm a jumble of emotions. Part of me wanted him to join me. Another part of me enjoys the alone time.

Washing off this whole, horrible event helps me feel more like myself. Dante enters the bathroom, silently closing the door. A plastic crinkling noise makes me crack open the shower door.

One corner of Dante's mouth lifts in a tired smile. "Asked one of the girls to grab a few things for you."

"Thank you," I whisper.

After stepping out of the shower, Dante wraps me in a fluffy towel and dries me with such gentle care, I almost cry. Wrapping the towel tightly around me, he leads me across the hall to his room.

"Gonna take a room upstairs, babe, so when we're here you can have your own bathroom," he murmurs as he shuts the door. I have no idea what he's talking about. There's an upstairs?

Exhaustion slams into me with the force of a brick wall once I'm safe in Dante's room. He helps me into one of his shirts, then pulls the covers back and waits for me to get in bed.

"Lie down, Karina." He nods at the closed bedroom door. "I'm going to lock that. You need anything, I'll be in the chapel. It's the big room right off the main bar area."

"Okay. Thank you."

Dante

KARINA'S out before her head even hits the pillow. Staring down at her, I don't know what to think. Something that almost feels like a conscience won't let me take advantage of her. I'm shocked I didn't fuck the hell out of her the minute we set foot in this room.

Even now, there's a strange disconnect stopping me from wakin' her up and stickin' my dick in her. She said he didn't hurt her. It doesn't stop my brain from thinkin' my girl's been violated and I should be takin' better care of her.

I cover her up and, as promised, lock the door behind me.

"That was fast," Romeo says with a snicker when I take my seat at the table.

The fact that I got nothing, signals I ain't in the mood to fuck around and Romeo gets down to business.

"Heard from our Mexican friends. Hemi ain't down there. Spoke to Bolt—"

I have to stop him there. "You bringing the Savage Dragons in on this?"

Romeo's not a fan of being interrupted. "Yeah. Thought they should keep an eye out for the little punk."

"They're more likely to give him shelter than hand him over."

Romeo shrugs. "You still gonna kill him?"

Here's where my supposed level-headedness comes in handy. "Depends. I ain't sittin' at this table with him again, I'll tell you that."

"Didn't expect you to, brother. We're still missing a package, though. It might be easier to get him to come in, if he knows you ain't gonna slit his throat first chance you get."

Wolf pipes up for the first time. "Call Tucker. He

should be out that way. Got connections to both Bolt's crew and Hemi."

"Yeah, was thinking that too," Romeo says. He whips out a burner, placing it on the table and leaving it on speaker for all of us to hear.

"You've reached Ken Rivers..." blood thunders through my head when I hear the name. Not exactly an uncommon last name, but that, combined with the fact I know Karina's dad drives a rig...

"What's wrong, Dante?"

My head tips up to find prez staring at me with a confused expression. "Nothin'."

We can't reach Tucker. Romeo moves to other club business and I'm havin' a bitch of a time sittin' still. I gotta talk to my girl. I need information from her.

He finally closes the meeting and asks me to stick around. When everyone leaves, he gets up and shuts the door.

"How's she doing?"

I'm surprised he gives a shit. "Resting."

"He hurt her?"

Now normally, I'd think Romeo was asking so he'd have something to get off on, but he seems genuinely concerned.

"She said no. But he left her fucking tied up and alone. She was terrified."

"Jesus. What a little shit. How'd we misjudge this fucker?"

"Don't know, brother."

"Fuckin' Tucker's the one who introduced me to him.

Vouched for the little fuck. Definitely need to have words with him. She tell you why?"

I cock my head at him. "Whaddya think? You heard him the night I laid his ass out."

"Yeah, but I thought he got over it. Been fuckin' Sadie ever since."

That's how out of it I've been. Haven't really noticed or given a shit about anything except my little bitch.

"You stayin' up here tonight?"

"Think so."

He nods. "Clubhouse will be packed. I'll come get you if I hear back from Tucker or anyone else."

"Thanks, brother." I stand and Romeo slaps my hand.

"Glad it ended well, Dante. That coulda gone real wrong."

That's what keeps nagging at me the most.

KARINA'S still asleep when I get back to my room. Someone turned the music up in the clubhouse, so I doubt she'll be able to sleep much longer. I slide in beside her and pull her tight to my chest. One of her breathy sighs later and my dick's twitchin' to life.

Never remember sleeping with a woman before she came into my life. Fucked plenty of them. Never let any of them stay long enough to *sleep*.

"Dante?"

"I'm here, baby girl."

"*Mmmm*."

She turns in my arms, her soft breath tickling my chest. It's impossible to fall asleep, but holding her calms me.

I'm hovering right at the edge of sleep when she whispers my name again. Shifts a little. Arches her tight little body against me. Her soft lips travel over my neck and down my chest.

"Dante, I need you."

My eyes snap open. Sleep's the last thing on my mind. "I'm here."

"Mmmmm."

I've got her naked in about five seconds. Dick free and in my hand in another two seconds. Pinned flat on her back under me a second later. She spreads her legs and hooks her feet behind my back. "Please."

Fuck me. I'm sliding into her tight, wet cunt a second later. We both groan as I let her adjust. I feel like I'm motherfuckin' home again.

CHAPTER FIVE

KARINA

THIS IS WHAT I NEEDED. Damn Logan for making me doubt Dante. Doubt *myself*.

"Harder, Daddy" I whisper against his ear.

"Fuck, baby girl, you tryin' to kill me?"

He pulls out, urging me to turn over and get on all fours. It's dark, but I don't need to see him. I just need to feel his warmth and protection surrounding me. Feel him inside me. We groan together as he fills me, teasing me with a few short strokes, before gripping my hips and pounding into me like crazy. His fingers twine in my hair, twisting and pulling me up against him. His mouth on my neck sends streaks of pleasure down to my nipples. It's as if he knows it too, because he loosens his grip in my hair. Both of his hands cup my breasts as he slows his frantic thrusting. Rough thumbs tease and roll my nipples until I'm panting and squirming.

"Please, please, please,"

Warm breath skates over my cheek as he bites at my ear. "What do you need, baby girl?"

"You."

"You got me. What else?"

One of his hands drops to my hip, then slowly slides down. His fingers brush my clit with feather-light strokes you wouldn't expect from a man so rough.

"More?" he rasps against my ear.

"Yes, please." I barely recognize my own voice, it's so close to begging. "Please, Dante."

A growl rips from his throat and he pulls out of me, nudging me on my back. Working his way down my body, he leaves a trail of kisses over my breasts, my tummy, and uses his big hand to open my thighs wide. Thick fingers dig in to my flesh, holding me the way he wants. His warm breath tickles over my sensitive flesh and I let out a whimper.

"You smell like fuckin' heaven, Karina."

My skin heats from his intense tone and the way he seems to be studying me. It's wrong, but also so right.

He brushes a finger against my clit and I jump, pushing into his hand. Oh, shit. His tongue flattens against me, sampling me again, and more needy crying noises ease out of me.

"Fuck me. You're the best thing I've ever tasted." His words vibrate against my pussy making me even crazier with need. He holds me open and attacks me with his tongue and lips, devouring me, until I'm bucking and squirming against his face. One finger drifts over my pussy, then slides inside, expertly finding that spot that makes me cry out and grind into his face even harder.

I'm barely finished quivering when he crawls back up

my body, lowering himself between my legs. I shiver as the head of his cock presses against me.

"Good, baby girl?"

"Oh, yes. Please, give me more."

"You want this?" he teases as he pushes in just enough to make me cry in frustration.

"Dante, stop teasing…"

His warm, rough laughter rumbles over me. "It's killing me just as much."

I bump my hips up. "Then fuck me."

He leans down, catching the sensitive skin of my neck with his teeth. "Easy, baby girl. Don't make me spank you."

"Maybe I want you to."

He finally has mercy and shoves all the way in then stops. "Christ, baby girl. I haven't had such lack of control since I was a teenager."

I'm not sure what he means, but I tighten and arch my back. He presses his hips into me, sinking further inside, but also pinning me down. "Don't. Fuckin'. Move," he growls against my ear.

My arms slide around his neck and I pull myself up so I can whisper in his ear. "Give it to me hard. Fuck me like you mean it. Like you were as scared as I was."

He draws back, and even in the dark, I can see his eyes searching my face. He pulls out, and then pushes back in, harder than before.

Closing my eyes, I fall back against the bed, arching my back, offering myself to him. His mouth covers my breast, sucking my nipple so hard pleasure zings straight through me. He moves to the next breast, giving it the same treatment, and I wriggle under him until he slams into me again. His slow, ragged breaths excite me even more. Each time he pushes in, he grinds himself against my clit then pulls out so slowly, dragging against the spot that feels sweetest.

"More." I barely get the word out before he rams himself home again. I gasp and moan in surprise, then giggle because it feels so amazing. Then he lays his big body over mine, so we're pressed together and he hammers into me hard and fast.

I gasp and his mouth covers mine, kissing me fierce and violent until I break and come apart under him again. This time he comes with me, and I feel every pulse and twitch as he fills me with his cum. Even as he's winding down, he keeps thrusting into me, milking every last throb of pleasure from my body.

He raises himself up on his hands and kisses my cheek.

"Karina? Baby? Why're you crying?"

"I'm so happy to be home."

Dante

I feel the same way. We're not home, but her home's with me. Wherever I am is where she belongs. I press my lips against her forehead and roll off her. "Yeah, me too."

She nuzzles her way under my arm until her head's on my chest. Warm breath drifting over my skin. I let her have a minute, until her breathing evens out. My arm flexes, giving her a quick squeeze. "We need to talk, baby girl."

She stirs, presses her hand against my chest and sits

up, tucking the sheet under her arms. Reaching over, I flip on the lamp beside the bed. It throws out a weak circle of light, but it's enough for now.

"About what?" she asks.

I slide myself up, so my back's to the headboard, and she scoots over with her back to the wall. "I need you to tell me everything that happened."

"But I already—"

"Karina." I use a sterner tone and her eyes widen. "Tell me everything he said to you."

"He said a lot of crazy stuff."

This is gonna be like pullin' teeth. Good thing I've got experience extracting information from reluctant sources. Bad thing is I can't use any of my usual methods on my girl.

"Tell me how you two first met."

She scrunches up her face as if she can't understand why I need to know that bit of history. I'm not sure either, but I feel like a giant piece of this puzzle is in her past.

"We lived next door to each other when we were kids. My mom…drank a lot. My dad was always on the road." Her shoulders lift and she glances at the door. "He made sure I got to school safe and would bring dinner over if my mother was too out of it to cook."

Christ, I hate hearing the shit she's been through. "And?"

"I don't know. I had a crush on him. I was a girl and he was a boy who was nice to me. My mother died when I was twelve and my dad actually stayed home for a while and took care of me. He didn't like how close we were, so Logan stayed away. But as usual, my Dad took off again."

She snorts and shakes her head. "I annoyed Logan until he said he was my boyfriend." She looks down at her hands, wiggling her fingers. "He was my first. But you know that."

"Yeah. When'd you break up?"

"Sophomore year? After he graduated." She sniffles and keeps her gaze focused on her hands. "We spent the summer together. It was the best summer of my life. He took me everywhere with him. Then at the end of the summer, he told me we were through. He was joining the MC and couldn't have a kid for a girlfriend."

It sounds cruel, but knowing what we put the prospects through, it was probably for the best.

"Of course, like a fool, I didn't believe him. I kept coming around his house." She shakes her head in disgust. "Leaving him these pathetic notes. He yelled at me. I still didn't get it. I caught him with another girl, and I just threw myself at him even worse."

I reach out and grab her hand, but it only makes her cry harder.

"I was an idiot. I see that now. But back then—"

"It's okay, baby girl."

"One or two nights after our last big argument, a man crept into my room. He…threatened me. Told me to stay away from Logan."

I bolt upright and tug her closer. "Who? What man?"

"I don't know. I couldn't see his face. I didn't recognize his voice. He reeked of smoke."

"Did he hurt you?"

She ducks her head so her hair falls forward, covering her face. "Yes."

I'm so fucking livid, the edges of my vision turn red. "Did he rape you?"

"No. Not exactly."

What the fuck does that mean?

I give her a minute to get herself together.

"He held me down…forced his…Dante, I can't do this. It's too embarrassing. I've never told anyone what happened that night."

"Karina. You've got nothing to be embarrassed about with me. Not ever. Someone hurt you and I want to know what happened so I can fix it."

"You can't—"

"Yes, I can. Now tell me." Is this the right thing to do to a traumatized girl? I have no fucking idea. Fuckin' the hell out of her for the last couple months was probably wrong too. Didn't stop me. And I ain't stupid enough not to know that most of the girls who hang around our clubhouse been through similar shit. Never stopped to think about it before. Long as they were of age and no one was forcing 'em to be here, I never gave a shit about their issues. My girl, though? I ain't kidding. Somehow, I *will* fix this.

"He…forced his fingers in me. Until he…got me off. Then he said since I could get off so easily for someone else, I obviously wasn't as in love with Logan as I thought I was, and I needed to find another boyfriend to take my mind off him. Threatened to come back if he heard one word about me sniffing around Logan again."

Jesus Christ, that's some fucked up shit. And this is from a guy who treated 'fucked up' as his personal motto.

"What else?"

She shakes her head. "Nothing. I stayed away from him. Kept my head down and my mouth shut. Maybe a week before you and I met, I ran into him with some girl on the back of his bike." Her shoulders twitch. "It made me so fucking angry."

"So you decided to get even with him?" Lucky for me. Were it not for that little run-in, she and I might not have met. Now that I have her, I don't know what the fuck I'd do without her.

"Yes. It was stupid. I'm so sorry, Dante."

"Nothing to be sorry for, Karina. You came clean. We talked it out. We're good." I'm slammed with the thought of just how innocent she is. Plot she came up with? Not many of the women I know would feel a hint of shame over it. My girl's still apologizing.

I'm so motherfuckin' *wrong* for her.

The worst part is, I don't care. She's mine now. No matter what.

CHAPTER SIX

DANTE

"What else can you tell me?"

She fidgets and blows air out her pursed lips. "I don't know. It was a long time ago. I tried so hard to forget."

"Just think. Anything?"

She leans back and closes her eyes. "He was big. Not as big as you, but in the dark, looming over me, he seemed huge."

"Okay."

"He had an accent. Not Spanish or Southern like around here."

That's interesting. And probably helps me cross a lot of people off my list.

"It reminded me of one of those mob boss accents, like on TV. I was so scared he was like some crazy mafia guy, come to cut my fingers off."

Neither of us laughs. In my head, I'm guessing she means a New York or Jersey accent. Know a few MCs in that area. Know one or two nomads from that area who do jobs like Karina's describing.

"That's good, baby. Thank you."

She nods but looks so damn lost.

Holding my arms out, I urge her closer and she crawls over the tangled sheets to throw herself against me, letting out a harsh sob. "I was so scared, because I was all alone. I made my dad get all new locks, but I used to be terrified when he was gone for long stretches."

Jesus Christ. Again I'm asking myself how the fuck anyone could abandon this girl? "Baby, what's your dad's name?"

She peers up at me, forehead wrinkling in confusion. "Ken, why?"

Fuck me. "Ken Rivers?"

"Yeah. Why are you asking?"

"No reason. Just thinking I ought to have a chat with him one day about the right way to take care of a daughter."

Her lips quirk up. "You don't have to do that. I'm safe now."

Hearing her say that is like a fucking knife twisting in my chest. I lean over and kiss her forehead. "Yeah, you are."

Before I can get anything else out someone knocks on the door. "Shit, give me a second."

She nods and rolls herself up tight in the sheet. I slip on a pair of sweatpants and find Sadie on the other side of the door.

"You said she needed some stuff?" She holds out two plastic shopping bags. "Nothing fancy."

"Thanks, Sadie. What do I owe ya?"

"Nothing. Luck took care of it."

I raise an eyebrow and she shrugs. Looking past me, she waves at Karina, and I take a step back. "Party goin' on, sweetheart, not as rowdy as usual, if you want to join us?"

"Thanks," Karina says and when I turn, I see she's blushing a couple different shades of red.

I appreciate Sadie making the effort to make my girl feel welcomed. "Thanks, Sadie."

After she leaves, I paw through the stuff. Fuckin' Sadie knows me well. I snort at the mini-skirts and the lack of underwear in the bags.

"You up to hangin' out there?"

"Sure. Whatever you want."

Yeah, I know she'll do whatever I want, but that's not what I asked. She reaches for the bag and pulls out one of the skirts. Her cute little nose wrinkles and she pulls out a pair of leggings. "Nah, just the skirt, baby girl."

Her wide eyes meet mine and one corner of her mouth curves up in a sly smile I'm not used to seein' on my girl.

Karina

WHEN DANTE TELLS me what he likes to see on me, the intense way he focuses his dark eyes on me, my insides turn to liquid heat. Slipping into the short, black full skirt without anything underneath feels wrong, but in a good way. The material is soft and when it swirls around my legs a wave of sexy confidence washes over me. Sadie included a thin red tank top. When I reach for my bra, Dante stops me.

"Wanna see those nipples poking through, babe."

For a second it's like trying to breathe underwater. "Dante, I can't—"

"Yeah, you can."

I can do anything if he says it in that voice. My knees weaken and he steps closer, until my nipples brush against his chest.

His hand grazes my thigh, pushing my skirt up, slipping between my legs. One thick, rough finger finds my pussy, rubbing slow and steady. "I think you like it."

I do.

Abruptly he stops. "Get dressed, or I'm gonna fuck you until you can't walk."

"Maybe I want you to."

His mouth tips up in a wicked grin. "I think you wanna go over my knee later."

He's right.

I slide the shirt on and try not to feel completely naked with my breasts bouncing under the flimsy fabric.

There's a pair of black ballet flats in the bag and I raise an eyebrow. "No hooker heels?"

"Nah, I'd rather have you barefoot, but not to run around here."

I'll have to keep that in mind.

The simmering look he gives me when I'm ready to go almost makes me want to stay in. But I'm curious and full of nervous energy. My stomach rumbles. Apparently, I'm also hungry.

When we're in the hallway, he pulls me close. "You

look perfect in my club's colors," Dante whispers in my ear.

"Red and black?"

His mouth curves into a soft smile I've only ever seen him use with me. "Yeah."

The main room is crowded. People yell to Dante, and I tuck myself against him as tight as I can.

He steers me to the bar and glares at one of the men seated there until he moves; then he fits his hands onto my waist and lifts me onto the stool.

"How you feeling, Karina?" The low gentle voice on my right belongs to Luck and my mouth pulls into a smile.

"Better."

He turns to Dante, who's taken up the space behind me, but left his hands on my shoulders. "Romeo's looking for you."

"Figured. Can you have one of the girls bring her something to eat and watch her while I go talk to him?"

"Yeah, no problem."

Dante squeezes my arm before leaving. Then I'm alone with Luck. Not that he scares me. The opposite really. In this whole scary place, he's the only one who *doesn't* frighten me.

"What do you want to eat?"

"I don't know. What are my options?"

"Anything."

I cock my head at him and he laughs. "Grilled cheese?"

"You got it." He turns and flags one of the nearly naked girls running around. She glances at me and smiles which is a nice change from the stink-eye I usually get.

"She's not going to spit in it is she?" I ask him after she leaves.

"Not if she knows what's good for her." He doesn't crack a smile when he says it. "Dante says you're finishing your senior year?"

For some reason, my cheeks heat up. "Yeah."

"Know what you want to do after?"

"Something in the medical field." I've been rethinking this a lot lately. In fact, before all the craziness with Logan happened, I wanted to talk to Dante about a chemistry class one of my teachers suggested I take over the summer.

"Nice. You must be smart." At first, I think he's teasing me, but he doesn't smile.

"Thanks."

The girl Luck asked to grab my dinner slides in between us and sets a plate down on the bar.

"Thank you."

"Need ketchup?"

"Yes, please."

Her mouth curves up. "Yeah, I can't eat 'em without lots of ketchup either. I'm Amy if you need anything around here, just let me know."

"Thanks, Amy."

I really am starving, so I practically ignore Luck while I devour my sandwich. "Amy's nice," I mumble at him between mouthfuls.

"Yeah. She's a good girl. Sadie, too. They both help out a lot around here."

I nod but I wonder if he's hinting that I should help around the clubhouse?

Dante

"Tell me you heard somethin'?" I ask as soon as I step into Romeo's office.

"Sort of." He jerks his chin at the chair across from his desk. "Have a seat."

A heavy sigh that doesn't conceal my irritation leaves me as I drop into the chair.

"Can you cut the dramatics, prez?"

One corner of his mouth tips up in a smirk. "Fuck you. Not all of us got to spend the afternoon in tight, young pussy."

"You're awfully obsessed with where I park my dick lately."

He smirks even wider, then drops his gaze to his desk. "Heard from a contact. Your girl's car was found near Willow Beach."

"You think he's headed to Vegas?"

"I don't know. Pretty fuckin' stupid if he is."

He's right. Romeo's connections in Sin City run pretty deep. "You think he headed somewhere else?"

"He's not dumb. Usually," he amends.

"I've got another problem. I'm pretty sure Tucker is Karina's father."

The shock on his face is more than I expected.

"That *is* a problem. I got personal business with Tucker."

Not a surprise that prez has some side action.

He shakes off whatever's bothering him. "Ain't a

problem. She's under our protection now. He can fuck right off, if he don't like it."

I'm real fuckin' glad he sees it that way. Makes my life easier. "What're we doing with Hemi?"

"Still got guys lookin' for him. Fuckin' sucks, we got no idea what he's drivin' now. Bolt's crew is gonna tow her car here so we can go through it."

"Sounds like a plan. Hey, I want to take one of the rooms upstairs."

"'Bout fuckin' time."

I smirk because it's always bugged Romeo that I don't give a shit about where I lay my head. His way of thinkin' is that officers of the club belong in the cushier rooms upstairs. I've never given a fuck. I ain't a part of this club for status.

"I'll put you next to me, so I can hear your hot lil' girl screamin' her head off when you're railin' her."

"No fuckin' thanks. I don't wanna be anywhere near your sex dungeon. Just want a private bath and bigger space so she's more comfortable when we're here."

Dick that he is, he places both hands over his heart. "What a gentleman."

"Fuck you." I tap his desk with my fist. "Need anything else from me?"

"No. Go take care of your girl. Old man like you probably has a hard time keepin' up with her. Let me know if you need script for some little blue pills." he says as he stands and rounds the desk.

"Nah, I'll leave those to you."

He walks me out into the main room and we stop to survey the clubhouse. Place is damn close to being one big drunken orgy. Half-naked and fully naked bitches everywhere. Only one bitch I wanna see. *Mine.*

She's still at the bar with Luck.

"You ain't worried about them hanging out together?" Romeo asks.

I actually stop and think about it. *No.*

One of our prospects approaches her with his player face on. Now, him? I'm ready to rip his arms off and beat him to death with them. Luck scares him away and Karina shines one of her innocent smiles at him. Now I can't stop thinking of the kinky shit I know he's into. Picturing him tyin' her up in all sorts of obscene positions, has my dick so hard I gotta stop and adjust myself. "Later, Romeo. Keep me up-to-date."

I don't wait to hear his answer.

Karina flinches when I wrap my arms around her waist, but then settles against me. "Hey, baby girl," I whisper against her ear.

She goes soft in my arms, tipping her head back to smile. "Hi. Missed you."

Fuck, she's sweet. Smells sweet too, and before I know what I'm doing, I'm rubbing my face against her neck and tugging at her earlobe with my teeth. Love the way her body trembles and her nipples perk right up under my touch.

I turn to Luck. "Was she a good girl?"

He chuckles. "Yeah." He's not laughing at my question, he's laughing at the way Karina has her eyes closed and lips parted because I can't keep my hands off her nipples or out from under her skirt.

Sucking at the skin below her ear makes her moan and I whisper, "Spread your legs."

Anxious eyes pop open and stare at me. "Dante?"

"No one can see." I turn and smirk. "Well, except Luck."

She leans farther back against me, spreading her thighs. "My baby girl's so fuckin' wet."

She whimpers and opens wider. "That's it. Close your eyes." I trace my way from clit to cunt and back. "Want you to come for me," I whisper against her skin. I draw lazy circles around her clit until she's panting hard. My other hand's cupping her breast, thumb rubbing over the thin fabric covering her nipple. This is torture on my dick. I'm so hard it hurts, but the exercise in self-control will do me some good.

My finger teases her pussy, then slides inside finding and rubbing the spot that will push her over the edge. Little sighs and moans pour out of her. Instead of my fingers, I wish my face was between her legs and my tongue buried in her cunt.

She cries out, her hands come up tightening around my forearms, then she's clenching around my finger, coming so hard she jerks and trembles in my arms. I press my lips to the side of her head. "Good girl."

Her eyes pop open and she gives me a soft smile.

Luck hands her a bottle of water, making her blush and look away.

"Hey, Dante, can I borrow your girl?"

I straighten up to find Sadie behind us. "Come dance with us, Karina," she says, then looks at me. "I promise I won't let anyone touch her." She holds out her hand while raising an eyebrow at me. I nod. Karina slides out of my grasp, wobbles on her feet a little, then adjusts her skirt and lets Sadie lead her to the dance floor.

"You ever try orgasm denial with her?" Luck asks as I sit down and signal Amy to bring me a beer.

"Fuck no. Why the hell would I do that?"

He shrugs. "It can be fun." His mouth curves into an evil grin. "For you. Not her."

"God, you're a sick fucker." I laugh and shake my head. We turn to watch the girls on the dance floor. Sadie's got her hands on Karina's hips and my girl's lookin' freaked out and hot as fuck.

Karina

SOMETHING FEELS off about the way Sadie's trying to be so friendly. Maybe she wants to embarrass me in front of the clubhouse? But then, all we do is dance. When one of the guys comes up and tries to touch me, she brushes him off.

"She's Dante's girl, don't touch," is all she has to say for him to back off. She crooks a finger at him. "I'm everyone's girl. Touch as much as you want."

As I'm flicking my hair off my sweaty forehead, two arms wrap around my middle. Dante.

"Need you, baby girl," he says against my ear. His low voice sends pleasant tingles all over my body.

Sadie's getting plenty of touching from her admirer, so I turn to face Dante. "You got me."

He tugs me through the crowd and down the hall. But we keep moving past his door. "Dante?"

"Wanna show you somethin'."

I like the feel of his big, warm hand holding mine, leading me where he wants to go, which is through a large steel door and up two flights of steps. We're in another hall with doors on either side. "Gonna take one of the rooms up here, so you're more comfortable," he says as he keeps walking.

He pushes through another door, and we're outside. On the roof.

The door slams shut behind us, and I jump. "Are we locked up here?"

"No."

The view up here takes my breath away, distracting me for a moment. Dante pulls me into his arms. "It's so pretty up here," I whisper as I look up at him.

"Not as pretty as you."

My mouth opens in surprise. Before I can say anything, he leans down and kisses me. His lips are firm, demanding access that I immediately give him. Even so, he grips the back of my head, holding me tight. His other hand slides down to cup my ass, pulling me into his body. I can't get close enough, and throw my arms around his neck.

When he finally breaks our kiss, his lips curl into an obscene smile. "Need my cock in you, babe."

All the air in my lungs rushes out. I can't respond. I'm too wound up. He doesn't need me to respond. Rough hands lead me to the low brick wall surrounding the roof. Abruptly, I'm facing the night sky…and whatever is three stories below us. The parking lot.

"Dante—"

His hands slide over my hips and fit into my waist. "Bend over and put your hands on the ledge," he whispers, then runs his tongue down my neck, while his hands lift my skirt. I moan when his coarse hands brush against my skin.

"Don't make me tell you again, Karina."

I'm shuddering from a mixture of fear and desire as I put my palms against the wall. Warm night air kisses my exposed skin, and desire drowns out my fear. His hands position my hips the way he wants them, and then run over my ass.

There's a blunt nudge against my pussy and I arch my back just a bit more so he can get the right angle. I whimper as he invades me. Something about this angle and the size of him is too much. My cries don't slow him down though. He presses in all the way. Big, rough hands keeping me in place. My mouth opens on a silent scream as he tilts me so I can take him deep.

"That's my girl," he grunts as he fills me over and over. The force of his thrusts makes my hands scrape along the cool, gritty brick. Fear that my arms will give out freezes my insides. I don't want to end up kissing the brick wall or falling off the roof.

"Rub your clit, baby."

"I...I can't. I'm scared."

My words stop him. His arms band around me, practically lifting me off the ground. "Dante!" I yelp as he resumes his furious thrusting.

"You think I'd let you fall, baby girl?" he whispers against my ear. "Think I'd let anything happen to my beautiful girl?"

Those words unravel me. All my burning need comes rushing up from the depths of my heart. To be held and wanted. And fucked. Hard. “No, daddy.”

“That’s right. Time for you to come.”

I can’t hold back. A shattering pulse of pleasure steals my breath and voice. He keeps fucking me straight through it.

Dante

Death by fucking. Not a bad way to go. Karina’s gonna kill me for sure, with her tempting pussy I can’t seem to keep my dick out of. Her gasps and moans as she comes around my cock are fuckin’ beautiful. Repeatedly her pussy clamps down, squeezing the fuck out of me. I give her a second, then pull out and turn her to face me. She’s so dazed, she sort of sways on her feet.

“What—”

I let go of her long enough to get my T-shirt up and over my head, then drop it on the ground.

“Get on your knees,” I order. Sweet fucking little bitch doesn’t even hesitate. Kneels so pretty and peers up at me. “Suck.”

Her nose wrinkles and she takes a tentative lick.

“Don’t need to work me up, baby girl. I said suck. Open wide.” My hands thread through her hair, holding her so I can shove my cock in her mouth, thrusting until I hit the back of her throat. I pull back and almost lose it as her lips and tongue stroke me. The wrinkled nose is too much to ignore.

"Taste yourself on my dick, baby?"

She nods and hums, the vibration traveling straight to my balls. "You like it?"

This time she shakes her head and hums. It's fucking hot and cute, and I'm gonna lose it any second. "But you'll do it 'cause I asked. Right, baby girl? You wanna please me?"

She whimpers and nods.

"Good girl." She keeps her eyes on me, swirls her tongue around the head of my cock. Brings her hands up and starts working me. She's trying to get me off as fast as possible. I want to fuck with her, and hold off. But I can't control myself from finding a rhythm, pushing in deeper each time.

"Fuck," I groan, filling her mouth with cum. I'm amazed I've got anything left after the way I've gone at her tonight. "Good girl," I whisper as she swallows everything. I help her up and she wraps her arms around me. We stay like that for a second, then she pulls away and hands me my shirt.

Neither of us says anything as we leave the rooftop and go downstairs to my room. I'm on her the second the door closes. Yanking that little skirt down her legs and ripping that thin tank top away from her breasts.

"Know why I wanted to come in your mouth, babe?" I ask as I pinch and rub her rock hard nipples.

"No," she gasps.

"'Cause I wanna bury my face in your pussy and didn't feel like eating my own cum."

She gasps, and then giggles at my filthy words. She

ain't giggling two seconds later when her naked body's sprawled face down over my lap.

"Someone said they wanted a spanking before," I whisper against her ear. She raises her ass in the air.

"Yes, please."

Fuck me.

Underneath my lust, some other emotion uncoils, burning a path to my chest. For a second, I suck in a breath at the sight of her perfect ass. Bared for my hand.

"Please, Dante," she whispers softly. Her cheek's pressed against the mattress and her big, blue eyes stare up at me. The muscles in her legs tense as I run my hand over the soft globes of her ass. Everything about my girl is soft, sweet, and perfect. She's everything a man like me should never touch. She shudders as I run my fingers down her spine and the tight line of her ass. She sighs the first time my hand comes down on her ass. I go slow, taking time to touch her in between smacks. She's got a soft smile on her lips when I really start laying into her ass. She whimpers and pulls her arms up under her, but never tries to get away. I keep alternately smacking both cheeks until they're glowing.

"Had enough, baby girl?"

"No."

I'm afraid if I keep at her much longer, I'll hurt her. And I don't think she has any idea when to say stop. That leaves it up to me. Running my hands over her warm skin does nothing to calm my raging erection. My hands cup her cheeks and spread her open. She tenses and I lay a sharp smack on her upper thigh. "My ass, Karina. Mine. Stay still."

She whimpers, but not from fear or pain. "I'm sorry."

"I know you are."

Wedging my hand between her thighs, I open her wider. "My girl's nice and wet from her spanking."

Her eyes close and she moans softly while I dip my fingers inside her. She jumps when I drag a finger up to her clit.

"Sensitive?"

"Yes."

I dip my fingers inside her again, spreading her wetness to her ass. "Wish I had your plug here. Need to fuck your ass soon."

"Oh…oh…oh." She's moaning and babbling as my fingers work circles around her tight little hole. "I…I… have to tell you something," she stammers out.

"What's that, baby girl?" I stop teasing her so she can get some words out.

"I lost the plug."

"Lost? How?"

Her face is almost as red as her ass as she squirms in my lap to see me better. "When he came to get me, he said we'd be on lock down so I grabbed it while I was packing. It's in the car with all my books and other stuff. I'm so sorry."

It's wrong, but I can't help laughing. "You were thinking of me, baby girl?"

"Well, yeah."

I lift her so she's sitting in my lap. My hand grips her chin, turning her to face me. Her mouth's open and I plant a hot wet kiss on her lips. She grabs my shoulders and takes the kiss deeper. Hungry groans fill my mouth and my hand goes to the back of her head, holding her still.

When I finally pull away, her eyes are glazed, lips red and swollen. "Are you mad?"

"No. Fuck, no. It's sweet and hot as fuck that you were thinking of pleasing me even though you must have been scared."

The corners of her mouth turn up.

I slide her off my lap and onto the bed. "Come on, time for bed."

She drops her gaze to my rock hard dick, straining to punch a hole through my fuckin' pants. "But?"

"You want my cock again?"

"I need to come." Somehow, when my little bitch whines, it's the hottest fuckin' sound in the world. Nothing. *Nothing* about her annoys me. How long will that last?

CHAPTER SEVEN

KARINA

On Sunday, Dante says it's safe to go home. Happiness bubbles through me at the thought. Although no one bothered me this time, I still don't like sleeping over at the clubhouse.

Returning to Dante's cabin feels weird. Less than forty-eight hours ago, I'd been abducted from the front yard.

Inside, the stench of burned chicken fills the house.

"Oh, shit, Dante!" I yelp, racing over to the kitchen. The crockpot shut itself off, but not before everything in it charred.

"I'm so sorry," I say, choking back a sob.

Dante's hands settle on my shoulders, pulling me back against his chest. "What are you sorry for, baby girl?"

"I could have burned the house down."

He chuckles and turns me to face him. Big, warm, rough hands cup my cheeks. "Karina, were you planning to be kidnapped?"

"No."

"Then don't apologize. We'll throw it out and I'll buy you a new one. Don't give a fuck about a goddamn crockpot. Just happy my girl's okay."

That's it. I'm done. I throw myself against him, linking my fingers behind his back and sob against his chest. His arms wrap around me, holding me just as tight, while his hands rub up and down my back.

"You're safe, baby girl. I won't let anything happen to you again."

We stay like that for a while. Then Dante sits me down in the living room and flips the television on. While I absently flip through the channels, he tosses the crockpot in the garbage. He joins me on the couch and settles his hand on my knee.

"I'm so happy to be home, Dante." The words feel fuzzy as they fall off my tongue. This is my home now, right?

One of his hands tugs at the ends of my hair. "Happy you're home. Your car should be back tomorrow."

"Really? How'd you find it? Did you find Logan too?" Why did he wait to tell me this until now?

He reaches up and caresses my cheek with the back of his hand. It's an awfully sweet gesture considering what he says next. "None of that's stuff you need to worry about."

What the hell? Did the club find Logan and kill him? I'm surprised how much the thought bothers me. I shouldn't care.

"Does Hemi have any other family?" he asks while I'm figuring out what to say.

My mouth opens, but I stop to think about my answer.

"I think he had an aunt that lived in Wyoming? He spent one summer up there after he first moved here."

"Remember the name?"

"No. But it was his dad's sister. I don't know if that helps."

He leans over and presses a kiss to my temple. "Yeah, baby, it does. Thank you."

"Thank God, I'll have my stuff back. All my books were in there. I don't know what I'm going to tell my teachers tomorrow."

"Don't tell them what happened. Don't talk about it with anyone. It's club business and we'll handle it."

Stung, I pull away from him. "Dante, I'm not stupid. I wouldn't do that."

"Okay. Not even your friends."

I nod but I'm still hurt he thinks I'm so dumb.

"I'll take you to school tomorrow and pick you up."

I don't know why, but this big, bad, older biker talking so casually about dropping me off at school seems so wrong. I let out a burst of giggles.

"What're you laughing at, baby girl?"

"Nothing."

He's still eying me. "Want you to concentrate on your school work. Don't have much longer until graduation, right?"

"Yeah." I hesitate for a second, then dive in. "Before all the craziness with Logan, I wanted to talk to you about something."

He turns, draping his arm over the couch, so he can face me. "What?"

I'm struck with an overwhelming crush of emotion

because I can't remember anyone—except Logan way back when—ever giving me their full attention like this. I have to swallow a few times before I open my mouth.

"Um, well…my physics teacher thought it would be a good idea for me to take some chemistry classes over the summer at the community college."

"Yeah?"

"Uh, is that…okay?" My cheeks heat up and I have to look away.

Dante places two rough fingers under my chin and turns me to face him. "My girl's pretty fuckin' smart, huh?"

"Wha…What do you mean?"

He snorts and looks away. "Nothin'. Fuck yeah. Take whatever classes you want. Why would you even ask?"

My shoulders lift and I glance at my fingers nervously twisting together in my lap. "I don't know. I thought maybe I should get a job. It's not right that I don't contribute anything—"

"Your job is goin' to school and makin' me happy."

The corners of my mouth twitch up. "Okay."

"You think you need a job for some life experience or some shit, go ahead." He snorts. "Only jobs I can help you find are in the club's titty bar—which ain't fuckin' happening—or Romeo's garage. That's not happening either."

And here's the other thing I wanted to talk to him about. "My teacher also suggested I volunteer at the children's hospital over the summer. I'm, uh, thinking about med school again."

His mouth curves into a smile. "That's great. Love the idea of fuckin' a doctor."

I have to blush and look away. "It's eight years—"

He shrugs. "When you're my age, you start realizing years go by pretty fast."

"I'm still thinking of going to state and the campus isn't as far."

"I got enough cash to send you wherever you wanna go."

Wow. Holy shit. That's—"Dante, I don't expect you to put me through school—"

From the way his forehead wrinkles and his eyes narrow, I think I insulted him. "That's why I want to do it. You *don't* expect me to. You *want* to pull your weight. Most women I've known don't have goals other than gettin' knocked up and finding some dude to live off of. You're smart. You got ambition. I know you think I'm just a filthy biker, but I respect that, Karina."

"You're not a filthy biker."

"Oh, yes I am, baby. Don't ever forget it."

Dante

I'm in love with this girl.

Fuck me to hell and back. Did I just offer fuck knows how many thousands of dollars to put this bitch through school? This ain't about her being the best fuck of my life anymore. This is something else. Unmapped territory.

The look on her face when she so nervously asked me

if she could take a class. Asked me if I want her to get a job. Twisted me the fuck up. I need to be the one to take care of this girl. Never in my life have I given a fuck about doing the right thing for anyone other than myself or my club.

"Come on, baby girl. Time for bed."

She gives me a questioning look, but takes my hand and follows me upstairs.

Words don't have much meaning to me. Showing her is better. She walks ahead of me into the bedroom and I wrap my arms around her, pulling her against my chest. She leans back, limp and content. Shadows fill the room, but I don't need light. I know her body in my fuckin' sleep.

My nose is in her hair, tongue flicking her ear. I slide my hand up her body loosely wrapping it around her neck. Her pulse flutters wildly against my skin. "Do you understand what I feel for you, Karina?"

She swallows, the sensation reminding me of other things. "I think so."

So sweet and unsure. My fingers slide under her chin, angling her face so I can brush my lips against hers. Her sigh makes me press harder, tasting her slow and deep. Her knees weaken and her hands wrap around my arms, sexy little noises come from the back of her throat. My dick's so hard I ache.

We shuffle to the bed with my hand at her neck and one arm around her waist. "The things I plan to do to you, little girl…"

"Anything," she whispers.

"What's that?"

"Do anything you want to me."

"That's dangerous."

"I trust you." She sighs and relaxes against me.

I release her and push her forward. "Take everything off and lie down."

I'm ready to come in my pants. Otherwise, I'd laugh at how fast she gets out of her clothes and into position. "Someone wants to be fucked."

She angles her head so she can see me and nods.

"Put your feet flat on the bed and spread your legs."

"What? Why?"

For one second, I take my eyes off her, so I can snap on the bedside lamp. She blinks, and even in the weak light, I see pink racing over her skin.

"Didn't you just say I could do anything to you?" She jumps at my sharp tone and plants her feet on the mattress. "Knees apart, Karina."

Too slow for my wild brain, she parts them. Curling one of my big, scarred hands over each knee, I shove them wider.

"You like when I put my mouth on your cunt, baby girl?"

"Yes, daddy." A growl rumbles through my chest and a shudder works down my body. Fuckin' *love* the way her voice sounds when she calls me that.

I take a step back, otherwise I'm going to lose it and bury my dick in her in the next two seconds. "Cup your tits for me. Pinch your nipples. Harder." I fire off each demand and she follows.

Her skin's bright pink, but she keeps doing as I ask. "Don't be fuckin' shy with me, Karina. Put one of your hands between your legs."

She's either gettin' into it or tryin' to entice me up there, because first she sticks her finger in her mouth, makin' a show out of sucking it. Slowly she trails her wet finger down the middle of her body, stopping short of where I want. "Touch yourself. Rub your clit nice and slow for me." Her fingers move a few more inches and she hisses when they land on their target.

"Good girl," I whisper. "Now slide your finger down between your lips." I fight off a groan as her fingers glide right over her glistening pink skin. "Perfect girl. So nice and wet."

She hums and waits for her next instruction. Glancing up, I take in her closed eyes and her other hand still playing with her nipples. "Push a finger in." My throat's so tight, I have to choke the words out. Her knees drop to cover herself and I wedge my arm between them. "Don't you dare hide from me. You're so fuckin' sexy right now."

Her eyes meet mine searching to see if I'm tellin' the truth. I run a hand over my aching dick. "Yeah, you're hot as fuck. Gonna have to cut these fuckin' jeans off me, babe."

The corners of her mouth turn up and she reaches out for me.

"No. Put your hand back on your tit and play with your nipples like you were doing. Good girl," I add when she does it.

"Now, slide that other finger in your slick little cunt. In and out. Nice and slow." Fuckin' perfect. "Do you like that, baby girl?"

"No."

"No?"

She's actually pouting.

"Bullshit. Your juices are running over your fuckin' ass cheeks."

"That's you," she mumbles.

"What?"

"That's because of *you*," she says louder. "I like when *you* touch me. I'm thinking about *your* big, thick, rough fingers inside of me and then your smooth, wide cock filling me."

Fuck me. She wins. I'm tappin' out. I whip my shirt over my head and somehow get my pants down without ripping my dick off. The little smirk she's wearing disappears when I hook my arms around her legs and drag her to me. "Think you're fuckin' cute, don'tcha?" I ask. Each word comes out clipped and broken because I'm shoving my dick in her as I say them.

"You're finally fucking me, aren't you?"

Where did *this* girl come from? It's fuckin' hot. I slide my arms under her and hook my hands over her shoulders to keep her still for the pounding her pussy's about to take. "You're a mouthy little bitch tonight, huh?" I mutter against her neck as I keep thrusting.

"Y…yes. Oh, fuck. Please don't stop."

A dozen images of all the dirty things I want to do to her flip through my head. I release her and pull out, standing so fast my head spins. "Stand up."

She whines and I wrap my hand around her ankle, dragging her to the edge of the bed. When she's on her feet, I turn her to face the bed. "Bend over."

That, she's happy to do. "You've been bad. I wanted to watch you finger-fuck yourself and you ruined it." I drop each word with enough force that she peers at me over her shoulder.

"I'm sorry."

A couple of quick, hard slaps on her ass later, she's dancing on her toes. "I'm sorry!"

Then I'm grabbing her hips and sliding home again. She claws at the sheets while I fuck her with ruthless strokes. "I don't think I should let you come, Karina. What do you think?"

"No." This time when she looks back at me there's a wobble to her bottom lip, like she might cry. Fuck, even that's a turn-on. "Please let me come, please," she's begging so hard she's close to tears. I just keep slamming into her harder, trying to get deeper. My hands grab, push and pull her ass, so I can get the best angle.

My balls are drawn up so tight it fuckin' hurts. A good hurt. I can't wait to shoot my cum in her. Underneath me, she's still moaning, begging, and whining. "You wanna come, do it in the next ten seconds. I'm damn close."

I take mercy on her and rub her clit in small circles until she bucks and shudders. That triggers me and a low, rough groan fills the room.

I'm still clutching a handful of her ass so I squeeze and she moans.

"Hey," she yelps when I give her a quick slap.

"Can't help it. Love that juicy fuckin' ass of yours."

She wiggles it in response and it makes me laugh. I crawl up her body, stopping to suck each nipple into my greedy mouth. "Kiss me."

She throws her arms around my neck and puts her mouth to mine gently. She pulls away and slicks her tongue over her bottom lip. "Thank you for letting me come."

The corner of my mouth curls up in a smirk. Her fuckin' orgasms are as much for me as they are her.

"Get ready for bed, baby girl."

Karina

My ass is actually sore the next morning as I straddle Dante's bike so he can drop me off at school. A sweet burn that reminds me of last night's activities.

He pulls up right in front as if he owns the place. Oddly, it makes me feel less out of place. It's early, so I have time to kiss Dante goodbye.

When we part, he puts his hand to my face. "Be at the clubhouse most of the day. I'll have a new phone for you this afternoon, but if you need me for any reason, call there first."

He hands over a piece of paper with the numbers for the clubhouse and Luck. For a second, I can't speak. Sure, my dad always left a number for me to call while he was on the road. But I had an emergency one time—a kitchen fire. Calling my dad hadn't gotten me a damn thing, except a "good thing the fire department got there in time."

Somehow, I know if I call Dante, he'll be there.

"Thank you."

He angles his head and stares at me, but we're interrupted by Athena who races over and throws her arms around my waist. "I've been calling you all weekend!"

She's jumping up and down, while still hugging the crap out of me. Dante's mouth turns up and he raises an eyebrow at my best friend's antics. "I lost my phone," I say as I tug myself out of her grasp. She rolls her eyes at me and then seems to notice Dante.

I make the introductions and it's predictably awkward since Athena stands there gawking at him like a moron. "So you're the white knight who's takin' such good care of my girl." She runs her gaze up and down his body. "Or knight in black leather."

Dante seems pleased and I want to yank Athena's hair out by the roots. Until he takes my hand and pulls me closer. "I like takin' care of her." Jesus. If he keeps looking at me like that, I'm going to skip school and go straight home with him.

Athena clears her throat. "So, mister big, bad, scary biker, when do I get an invite to party at your clubhouse? You got any brothers as hot as you?"

Dante choke-laughs at my friend's brazen question and I smack her arm. "What's the matter with you?"

"How old are you, Athena?" Dante asks her.

She opens her mouth to lie through her teeth so I answer for her. "Seventeen. She won't be eighteen until the day after graduation."

"Bitch," she grumbles at me.

Dante points a finger at her. "You're trouble. Tag along with Karina *after* graduation." He turns to me. "I'll see you later, baby girl."

Then he's turning over the bike, twisting the throttle, and speeding away.

The smirk on Athena's face is begging for a bitch slap.

"Baby girl?"

"Yeah." While I got here early, now I'll be late if we don't hurry inside. Of course, I have to drag Athena, who wants to ditch.

"Come on. Fritz will be here."

"Okay. Okay."

Dante

ME AND MY hard-as-fuck cock are waitin' at the curb for Karina at three sharp. I watch countless kids go by—none of them my girl. A flash of blonde hair catches my eye. Athena. I have to jog across the yard to catch up to her.

"Athena?"

She's startled, but smiles when she turns and sees me. "What's up?"

"Where's Karina?"

"I don't know. The Vice Principal's office called her down during physics. I haven't seen her since."

"Shit. What the fuck for?"

"No idea." Her brow wrinkles. "She said you were replacing her phone? We planned to catch up tonight."

Absently, I pat the pocket where Karina's new phone rests. "Yeah."

"She's probably up for Salutatorian."

"What the hell is that?"

The little gash has the nerve to roll her eyes at me. "Second in our class. She's super-smart."

Damn. Why didn't she tell me that? "No shit."

"Yeah, she'll have to make a speech at graduation."

Fuck, I'm proud of my girl. "And?"

Athena shrugs. "She doesn't really like public speaking." She holds up her thumb and finger a millimeter apart. "I know she's been slacking off just enough to knock herself out of second place."

My girl's clever.

"Do you want me to go try to find something out?" she asks.

"Do ya mind?"

She ignores my sarcasm and eyes me up and down. "Yeah, you should definitely wait out front. Where's your bike?" I point to the front of the school and she follows me. As we're rounding the corner, Karina comes flying down the front steps, but stops when she sees my bike. She turns our way and somethin' ain't right. Red-faced and red-nosed like she's been crying. What the fuck?

"Karina! What's wrong?" Athena yells and goes runnin' down the sidewalk.

My girl's mumbling, "Nothing, nothing," when I reach them.

She throws herself against me, wrapping her arms around my waist. "What's the matter?"

"Nothing. Can we please go home?"

Pushing her away, I stare into her eyes, but she turns away from me. In front of the school and her friend ain't the place to talk, so I nudge her toward the bike.

"Karina, call me later, please? Or I'm going to worry about you," Athena pleads as Karina gets on behind me.

"I will, promise."

Athena narrows her eyes at me and raises an eyebrow.

I read her loud and clear. Little fuckin' ballbuster, this one is. She definitely needs to stay away from my clubhouse.

Karina wraps herself around me and we head home.

As soon as we're in the house, I take her by the hand and sit her down on the couch. "Tell me what's going on."

Tears roll down her cheeks. "I'm so sorry."

"For what? Talk to me. Athena said you got called to the Vice Principal's office. Why?"

She buries her hands in her face and sobs. If I don't get some answers from her soon, I'm gonna go back to that fuckin' school and burn it to the ground.

"Karina," I snap. My sharp tone dries up her tears and she faces me. "Tell me, now."

She takes a few deep breaths. Her quivering bottom lip sends a jolt of rage through me. Whoever upset my girl is gonna fuckin' pay for it. "I got called down there, because someone made an anonymous call to the school and told them I was living with you."

"So?"

"So, Mr. Hackett said he's going to call DCS and have them investigate you."

I laugh without much humor. This *Hackett* doesn't know who he's messing with or what he just brought down on himself.

"I'm so sorry, Dante. Please don't be mad at me. It wasn't my fault. I didn't tell him—"

"Hey." I reach out and pull her into my arms. "I know it's not your fault. I ain't mad at you."

"But—"

"Honey, I don't give two fucks about some high school suit or some stupid agency. Where were these assholes when your dad was out on the road for days at a time, neglecting you?"

"I don't know."

"You let me worry about this, okay? I don't think it's an issue. You're eighteen. You can live wherever you want. But if it makes you feel better, I'll run it by the club's lawyer, okay?"

She sniffles and finally smiles. "Yeah."

"Anyone comes to the house, I'll deal with them. Now put it out of your head."

She glances down at her book bag and nods.

"Before you start your homework, I want to talk to you. Athena told me about you being second in your class, but purposely trying to drop your grades so you don't have to give some speech?" My words are teasing but her jaw drops and she shakes her head.

"I was not. She's such a liar. It doesn't matter now anyway. Mr. Hackett said I couldn't be Salutatorian, because I have 'poor moral character.' Even if I have the GPA, he won't let me speak at the ceremony. He threatened to call any college I apply to and inform them of my "behavior."

Seems I ain't gonna be throwing Mr. Hackett the beating I was planning. No, I'm gonna be throwing him for a cement block nap in a fuckin' lake. It's a good thing I've got years and years of training myself to stay completely still when I'm raging inside.

"He tell you who called?"

"No. He said a concerned neighbor."

That could mean anything and nothing.

"Dante, you think it was Logan? Another attempt to break us up?"

Yes, that's exactly what I think. "It's possible," I say carefully. "Maybe your dad?"

She shakes her head. "Maybe. I never told him who I moved in with though."

Somehow, I bet her father already knows. "I need you to call him for me tonight." I pull her new phone out and hand it to her. "He should know that you're okay."

I honestly don't give a shit if the father knows she's okay or not. No real man neglects his daughter the way he's neglected Karina. As far as I'm concerned, he's lost the right even to be her father.

Suddenly, her hand tightens around my forearm. "Dante," she squeaks out in a panicked voice. "Logan said… When I told him about the man who hurt me. He swore up and down he didn't know anything about it. He…he suggested my dad did it. He also said my father was the only reason he broke up with me. My dad didn't like Logan being part of your MC. But then, he said my father is the one who introduced him to you guys. Do you know my dad?"

Fuck me. "Why you just telling me this now?"

She shakes her head, her question about my relationship to her father forgotten—for the moment. "I don't know. We got distracted at the clubhouse and I forgot until just now."

"Tell me exactly what he said."

She wrinkles her nose. "I was so scared, I don't know if I can remember everything. He said he needed time. He wanted to earn money with the club to buy a place for us.

That my dad threatened him to stay away from me. But that's bullshit because Logan knew my dad was never home."

"Babe, prospects don't earn much money and they ain't got no time to hold down another job. He's been living at the clubhouse—"

"Yes, that's what he said, that I couldn't live there with him. But he could have explained this to me instead of being so mean."

Yeah, a real man woulda figured something out. Not broken her heart, and left her all by her fuckin' self when he knew damn well how shitty her home life was. Fuckin' Hemi's ten times the douchebag I thought he was.

"All right, call your dad. And don't forget to call Athena later. Actually, can she give you a ride after school tomorrow?"

"I don't know. Probably. Why?"

"Your car should be ready. I won't be able to get there on time. But if she could drop you off at Romeo's garage, that would work. I'll meet you there."

"Okay."

"Go ahead. Call your dad."

I stay right where I am so I can listen to the call. Unfortunately, the fuck doesn't answer and it goes to voicemail. "Hi, Dad, it's me, Karina. I, uh, just wanted to check in. Haven't heard from you in a little while. I wanted you to know I'm good and make sure you have my new number."

She rattles off the number and then hangs up. "Typical," she says. "He's not much of a talker."

While she calls her girlfriend, I get up and make us

some food. Her girlish chatter is nice background noise in my house and I stop what I'm doing to watch her. She catches me staring at her and smiles. A few minutes later, she hangs up and joins me.

"You didn't have to get off the phone."

"Oh, I thought you were annoyed I was taking so long."

Jesus. I cup her neck with my hand and run my thumb over her cheek. "You never annoy me."

Her lips twist into a frown, like she doesn't think that's possible.

"I mean it, baby girl. Like having you here. I never really spent much time here before. Mostly stayed at the clubhouse. But I like coming home now." Now that it actually feels like a home. Because of her. But I keep that extra-mushy shit locked down.

She looks away and I can tell she still thinks I'm full of shit. "It ain't about fuckin' you either. I can do that at the clubhouse."

Fire's flashing in her eyes when she turns back my way. "I know."

"Good. Now help me finish dinner."

CHAPTER EIGHT

KARINA

I DON'T EVEN WANT to go to school the next morning. But Dante forces me out of bed and tosses me in the shower.

"I thought bikers were anti-school," I whine while he watches me shower.

"I ain't the one going. You are," he answers with a smirk. Not even some seductive teasing with my shower puff interrupts his mission.

"Can't let those fuckers win, Karina. You gotta go in there with your head held high."

When he pulls up to my school, I groan when I see the three bitches clustered on the front steps.

"What's wrong, baby girl?"

"Nothing. That blonde one? Called me biker trash yesterday. She's an uppity bitch."

Dante narrows his eyes and glares at the girls. "That Addison Turner's daughter?"

Now it's my turn to narrow my eyes. "Yeah, Jayne. Why?"

"She looks just like her mama. Next time she hassles

you, you let her know her mama's been fuckin' biker trash behind her daddy's back for years."

"What? Who?" God, please don't let it be Dante.

"Slim. You ain't met him yet."

"Well, thanks for the tip. You made my day."

The corner of his mouth curls up in a sexy smirk. "Glad to help. Don't let anything get you down today. You got a few more months and then this place is history."

Shit, is this big, scary biker giving me feel-good advice? "Thanks, Dante," I whisper.

He takes off and I stare after him, wishing I were still on the back of his bike.

"Hey!" Athena yelps as she's running over the grass. She's out of breath by the time we catch up to each other.

"Did I miss hot, scary, biker man?"

"Yes."

"Still need me to drop you off at the clubhouse today?"

"Not the clubhouse. His friend's garage."

"Oh, poo."

I roll my eyes, because she says the weirdest shit sometimes. "The president of the club owns it. He's hot, but way too old for you," I tease, because I know it will drive her nuts.

"Old like your guy old? Or really old?"

"I don't know. I think he's older than Dante. He's kind of a pig though."

She waves her hand in the air. "Meh. Got enough of that around here. At least high school boys can still get it up."

"Yeah, but they don't last a minute," I snark back.

Jayne and her friends are gone by the time we reach

the stairs. Even though Dante handed me some fantastic ammunition to hurl back at her, I'd prefer to skip any more drama today.

Although I keep repeating Dante's advice to "keep my head up" all day, it's not easy. Especially when I pass Mr. Hackett in the hallway and he sneers at me like something that overflowed from his toilet.

Dante

"Luck, need you to gather some intel on someone for me," I ask first thing when I stroll into the clubhouse after dropping Karina off.

"Yeah, whatever you need."

"Hackett. VP at the high school."

He cocks his head and gives me a curious stare. "Okay." He doesn't question me though. That's not how this brotherhood works.

While he's busy gathering information for me, I check in with Romeo to see where he's at with Karina's car.

"Nothin'," he says. "Unfortunately the little fuck wasn't dumb enough to leave any clues."

"Of course," I mutter.

"You still meeting with Hade?"

"Yeah, at two. Karina's friend's droppin' her off at your shop to pick up her car. You gonna be there?"

"Should be."

"Good. I don't want anyone hassling her."

His mouth tips up into a cocky smirk. "Including me?"

"Especially you."

That makes his grin wider for a brief second. Then he turns serious. "How is she?"

"Okay."

"You get any more info out of her?"

"He's got an aunt in Wyoming. I've got a contact running that down."

"Good. You still up for Thursday's trip?"

I'm not really in the mood for a run to Santa Fe, but I'm the only one who can get the job done quickly. Plannin' to ask Luck to watch Karina, but I ain't discussing that with Romeo. "Yeah. Won't take long."

He nods and picks up a key. "Room upstairs is all ready for you two lovebirds. Even had the prospects move your stuff up there."

I arch a brow, because he knows I ain't keen on people touchin' my shit. Not that I keep anything important here, but still.

"Except your bed. Figured you'd want something with a stronger headboard to tie her down to."

"Jesus, you're a fucking asshole."

"Just tell me on a scale of one to ten, how fucking crazy is she in the sack?"

"Would you knock it the fuck off?"

"Shit, you're really serious about her?"

Seriously fucking annoyed with my president is what I am. "Yes."

He sits back in his chair with a sigh. "How do you think that's gonna work? She's a fuckin' kid."

"What's it to you?"

He stares at me for a minute as if he's trying to figure

out what to say, then lets another cocky smirk loose. "Don't wanna see you get your heart broken, brother."

"Yeah right, dick."

He finally stops prying into my love life and we discuss how things need to go down Thursday. When we're finished, he walks me out into the main room.

"I gotta head to the shop. Need anything, call me."

He takes off and I go meet Luck at the bar. "What'd you find out?"

Luck's got a photographic memory. Makes him perfect for jobs like this. He never needs to write down an address, or anything else incriminating. "Lives in a nice area north of Thunderbird."

"Neighbors?"

"Yes. But not too close."

"Family?"

"Son's in college. Wife left shortly after the son."

I nod, thinking over my plan. "You wanna come with me?"

"Yeah, whatever you need, brother."

Cracking my knuckles, I stare at Luck so he understands what I'm looking for. "Need to have a conversation with him. Threatened my girl yesterday and threw some other bullshit on her."

He raises an eyebrow. "Karina? Why?"

"He got an anonymous tip 'bout her living with me. Told her he was gonna call protective services or some stupid shit. She was in fuckin' tears when she came home."

Luck's face darkens. "Motherfucker."

"Yeah. Also said some shit about not letting her speak at graduation because of her 'low moral character.'"

Now, Luck's really pissed. I knew he'd be the right guy for this job.

"You're thinking Hemi's the one who tipped him off?"

"Yeah, that's the other reason I want to have a chat with him."

Luck snorts at the word "chat." Any talk we have with Hackett's gonna involve my fists and his jaw. "I got a meet with Hade, get the schedule, and do a pick up. Then I'm meetin' up with her at Romeo's shop."

The corner of Luck's mouth twitches.

"Yeah, I don't want her alone with him longer than necessary. Let's meet here at eight and ride to Hackett's together."

"You got it."

CHAPTER NINE

KARINA

It was total wishful thinking on my part that Athena would just pull up and let me out at Romeo's. Nope. After her last class, she went to the trouble of changing into a pair of short-shorts that would make Daisy Duke blush.

"Really?" I ask as she approaches.

"What? It's hot out." She grins wide and devilish. "Don't roll your eyes at me."

A kid I recognize from school and the clubhouse greets us when we get to Romeo's shop. "Hey, Karina, right? Romeo's inside. Dante called and said he's on his way." My heart kicks when he says Dante's name. He only dropped me off at school a few hours ago, but I miss him.

My gaze is drawn to the open door to the shop's office. With his arms braced against the doorframe, Romeo fills up the entire space. He really is a good-looking guy. He knows it too, which somehow makes him less attractive.

"Well, hey there, little Karina. Who's your pretty friend?"

Athena glows from the compliment, but she's too

tongue-tied to respond. “Romeo, this is my best friend, Athena.” I’m not sure how to introduce him. Dante’s friend? The president of the Iron Bulls MC? I’m saved by Romeo introducing himself.

“You go to school together?” he asks.

I want to figure out a way to work in that she’s only seventeen, but it seems sort of inappropriate. And honestly, it’s not my problem.

The rumble of Dante’s bike draws all of our attention to the front entrance. The galloping of my heart is nothing compared to the fluttering in my tummy when he gets off his bike and removes his helmet. His eyes find mine right away. My body’s compelled to run to him, but I’m afraid of embarrassing myself in front of Romeo and Athena, so I keep cool.

Cool only lasts a few seconds. The way his body moves as he swaggers my way. The sexy smirk. His deep voice when he calls out, “Hey, baby girl.” My feet are headed in his direction before my head knows what’s going on.

I close the distance between us by throwing myself against him. His arms wrap around me and our mouths meet. Romeo’s catcalls and Athena’s giggling are like a bucket of ice water over our heads.

“I missed you,” I whisper when we part.

His nose brushes against mine. “Me too.”

Panties. Soaked.

He loosely wraps his arm around my shoulders and steers me to the garage. Romeo snickers, then turns his attention on Athena. Dante seems to remember she’s still here too. He lifts his chin at Romeo. "Find anything wrong with it?"

"Nope. No clue."

Dante opens the door and pulls out my backpack. He hands it over with a knowing smile and my cheeks flame. I'm also sickened remembering being trapped in the car with Logan, afraid of what he might do to me. The slamming of the car door makes me jump and then Dante's wrapping his arms around me. His lips brush against my ear. "You okay?"

I nod and shake my head at the same time like some sort of cracked-out bobblehead doll.

"On second thought, I think I'm gonna find her a different car," he says to Romeo. His eyes meet mine. "Want to make sure my girl's safe."

Athena's eyes are wide. But for once, she keeps her mouth shut.

"Yeah, I can help you out. What were you thinking?"

"Maybe a small SUV." Dante runs the back of his hand over my cheek. "Does that sound okay?"

"Whatever you think is best."

He nods then glances at Athena. "Do you mind giving her a ride home? Maybe you two can hang out together for a while?" He flips open his wallet and hands me a couple bills. "Grab some pizzas or something."

"Okay."

"I've got a thing tonight. Won't be back until around ten."

I wonder what the "thing" he has to do is, but I'm not going to ask in front of Athena and Romeo.

"Wow," Athena sighs when we're back in her car. "He really…he's amazing."

"Who?"

She cuts me a look. "Your man. You know I've been worried he was like some creepy older dude taking advantage of you, but he's so…nice. Well, nice for a big, scary biker dude."

I can't help chuckling at the way she sees him.

We decide to look for prom dresses. Well, Athena decides I need a prom dress. She's had one burning up space in her closet since freshman year.

"I don't even know if I want to go to prom," I moan as she drags me into a floofy bridal boutique. "Why are we here?"

"You want a nice dress, not some cheap, flimsy thing."

"Why? I'm only wearing it once."

She gives me a look like she's thinking of choking me. "Here," she says, thrusting a hideous blue and nude lace monstrosity of a dress at me. "This is totally your color."

"That looks like some sort of pageant dress. No fucking way," I whisper loud enough that the sales girl glares at me. *Oops.*

We finally settle on a sleeveless, sky-blue lacy dress. The skirt reaches my knees and is the only dress in the store with a high enough neckline to keep my tits covered.

"So much material for a biker girl," Athena teases me as I model it for her. "Is Dante taking you?"

I can't help laughing. "No way. Why would he go to a high school prom?"

"Uh, 'cause he's your boyfriend?"

Boyfriend. "There's nothing 'boy' about him."

She lets out an exasperated snort. "Whatever." Her eyes sparkle with amusement.

Dante

Luck's dressed in traditional bad guy black and waiting for me outside when I pull up to the clubhouse. We don't bother wearing our cuts. This matter's personal.

He drives, while I rifle through my duffel bag of interrogation toys. My fists are lethal enough, but I enjoy the visuals.

Luck's intel was good. The VP's car sits in the driveway. No other neighbors in sight. Even so, we park away from the house and stay away from the road.

I don't bother with pleasantries like knocking. After circling the house, we determine Hackett is alone and in the kitchen. The explosion of glass shattering around the back door gets his attention; but he's so stunned, so unused to anything interrupting his perfect life, he just stands there gaping at us as we burst in the house.

I didn't bother covering my face. He's gonna know in two seconds why I'm here and who I am.

I point to one of the dining room chairs. "Sit."

"What do you want? I can give you money."

These fucks always think it's about money.

"Sit the fuck down."

He sits. Luck binds him to the chair and I crouch down in his face.

"You and I have some business to discuss, Daniel."

"Who are you?"

My fist connects with his jaw, snapping his head back. I barely feel it, but he acts like I put a bullet through his knee.

"Shut the fuck up. Who called you about Karina Rivers?"

He spits out blood and shakes his head. "What? This is about a student?"

For a smart guy, this fucker's pretty dense. Another pop motivates him to stop dicking around.

"I don't know! It was a man. We didn't speak long."

"You get a number from him?"

"No. Like I said, we didn't speak for very long."

"Enough that you upset my girl and said some nasty shit to her."

His eyes widen and he shakes his head.

"Don't bother fuckin' lying."

"I wasn't aware of what she's been up to."

"Oh, and what's that?"

"The man said she was whoring herself out to the Iron Bulls. Is that where you're from?" he asks.

Luck must be feeling left out. He smacks Hackett on the back of the head. "Don't worry about us."

At least that poor moral character comment makes more sense. Maybe I won't kill him after all. "Karina's no fuckin' whore. She's *my* girl. She ain't under age, so you threatening her with calling children's services in was bullshit."

"The caller said—"

"I don't want to fuckin' hear it. You could have easily looked that shit up. Don't ever threaten her again."

"I'm sorry—"

"Shut up. Here's what's gonna happen. You're gonna stay the fuck away from her." Asshole's nodding before I even get the first condition out. "You're calling me immediately if you hear from this prick again. And you're gonna find out his name and get me a number."

He shakes his head and I grip his hair in my hand and yank his head up. "Finally, and most importantly, if my girl has the grades she speaks at that graduation. And you'll write her a glowin' fuckin' recommendation to any college she applies to."

"Yes, of course." He focuses on his lap, as if he hasn't been staring at my face for the last half hour. "You're not going to kill me?"

"Not tonight."

CHAPTER TEN

DANTE

"What a fuckin' pussy." Luck's shaking with laughter while we drive away from Hackett's house. I explained in detail what would happen if he ran his mouth. We left him tied to the chair, but he should be able to work himself free in an hour or two.

"You gonna tell Karina she doesn't have to worry?"

"Nope. No reason to bring her into any of this. Less she knows the better."

He nods, but doesn't seem to agree with me. Doesn't matter. "I need another favor, brother."

"Okay."

"Gotta do that Santa Fe run Thursday. I'm still not comfortable leaving Karina alone with that fuck still out there."

He glances at me and in a wary tone asks, "And?"

"Can you stay at the cabin and watch her for me?"

"You want me to babysit your girlfriend? Why not just have her stay at the clubhouse?"

"Seriously? Come on, you're the only one I trust."

"Yeah, okay. Isn't she gonna think it's weird?"

"Doesn't matter."

We part ways at the clubhouse. Do I feel bad asking him to do something I should really ask the prospects to do? Not really. I barely trust them to watch my bike. I sure as fuck ain't gonna trust them with something as precious as my girl.

The house is dark when I pull up and a lick of concern brushes me. Pulling out my phone, I see Karina's sent me a few texts. The last one is the best.

On my way home.

She walks in a few minutes after me, with a big garment bag trailing over her arm.

"I'm so sorry, Dante, were you here long? I tried to text you a bunch—"

I gotta cut off her breathless rush. "Calm down, baby girl. It's fine. You two have fun?"

She relaxes, and it bothers me that she's—what? Scared I'd be mad at her? Her eyes roll and she sets her bags down on the end of the couch. "No. She made me go dress shopping."

I can't help laughing. Thought girls loved that shit. "Got a prom dress?"

"Yeah."

"Can I see it?"

"You want—?"

"Yeah, I want. Show me."

The simple rustling of the plastic dress bag gets me hard. "Show me, baby girl," I say again in a lower voice.

She turns, a question on her lips, but when she takes me in, she gets it.

She moves to go upstairs.

Okay, maybe she didn't get it.

"No. Clothes off. Right where you are."

"Oh," she breathes out, so soft I almost don't hear it.

Slowly, she works her shirt over her head. She's too flustered to be sexy about it, and that makes it even hotter.

Karina

"Clothes off right where you are."

When Dante growls out those words, my belly drops. My mouth's so dry. I can't force any words out. Good thing my hands are ahead of me. Even as my legs tremble, I'm working my shirt up over my head and sliding my shorts down my legs.

"Nice," he encourages.

With my eyes still on his, I reach behind me, hook my fingers into the garment bag, and work the dress loose.

"Get shoes too?" he asks.

"Yeah."

"Put 'em on."

This time I have to turn and I put a lot of effort into bending over the end of the couch and slipping into the shoes. Behind me, Dante chuckles softly. "You're sexy as fuck, babe. No extra wiggling required."

Biting my lip, I shimmy into the dress and turn. A soft gasp escapes me. Dante's almost right in my space. He's so big I don't expect him to move so silently.

But there he is.

"Fuckin' beautiful, baby girl."

Heat stings my cheeks. His hand reaches out and he traces the high neckline with one finger. "Are you excited?"

I don't think he's asking about the dance. "Yes."

"Turn around." Oh, God, the things his low, rough voice does to me.

My body shakes as I turn and position myself over the end of the couch. Ass up, legs wide. It's automatic and I'm filled with pride at the way he sucks air in and slowly lets it out behind me. "You know just what I want."

"I try."

"Well, you're damn good at it."

A light breeze grazes my legs as he flips the dress up. Thick, rough fingers hook into my panties and drag them down my legs, the soft cotton brushing against my already sensitive skin. He leaves them at my knees and grabs my hips, runs his hands over my ass, up and down my back. Patiently, I wait while he decides what he wants to do to me. His hands drift lower, then one thrusts between my legs, rough, yet somehow gentle.

I gasp and push back against him. Two fingers thrust up, tight and hard. A soft cry of shock and need leaves me.

"Drenched. You want to come on my fingers, baby girl?"

"If you want me to."

I get a soft pop on my ass. "I asked what *you* want."

A strangled cry tears out of my throat. "That *is* what I want." He keeps working his fingers faster, harder until I'm whimpering. "Make me come, daddy."

"Fuck," he growls. "Stay still."

His hands leave me for a second, and I keep myself

still. His hands grip my hips again, and he drives into me, savage and hard. My body burns in all the places where our skin touches.

"Don't come yet, baby girl," he warns.

His hands slide up, yanking the zipper down. He pulls me up long enough to work the dress off and toss it on the couch, then he's back to thrusting and teasing me.

"Tell me when you're close."

Close. I'm dancing right on the edge. "I'm close," I whimper.

He slows and rubs his hand in big circles over my back. "My girl's bein' so good."

Even though he's moving at a lazy pace, I'm still close. "Daddy." This time I whisper it as a warning. His hands slide under me, tugging and pinching my nipples. "Please," I beg as he keeps grinding into me.

"Fuck, I can't say no to my baby girl," he whispers against my neck.

Still, I wait. He didn't exactly say *yes*.

His hands tighten around my waist, and he pounds into me recklessly. "Okay, baby. Give it to me."

Two more strokes and I come. Then I lose track of how many times as each ripple of pleasure rises to a wave crashing into me, knocking the breath out of my lungs.

With one final, violent thrust, he comes. Hands still holding me, his thrusts slow to lazy sliding. Then he's covering me with his body, pressing me into the couch. His lips trail over my shoulder, burning a path to my neck and finally my cheek. My eyes drift open. One of Dante's hands rests next to me on the cushion. I let out a soft cry when I spot the torn skin on his knuckles. "Dante, are you okay?"

He shifts, taking his weight off me. "Yeah. Am I crushing you?"

"No." I run my fingers lightly over his hand. "You're hurt."

Behind me he stands, and pulls me up. "It's nothin'. But it's sweet the way you're worried about a few scrapes."

I'm not sure why, but I'm overcome with a cloud of anxiety and…something else. Turning, I throw my arms around his neck, clinging to him. "I couldn't stand it, if something happened to you," I whisper.

He hesitates, and then hugs me just as tight. "I ain't goin' anywhere, baby girl."

We leave everything downstairs. After cleaning me up, he tucks us into bed. My head's resting on his chest when I ask, "Did you have a good night?"

He seems surprised. "Yeah, baby girl. Much better once you got home."

That makes me happy.

"Athena was surprised you're not taking me to prom," I blurt out. Why did I say that?

He's silent. "That wouldn't be a good idea," he finally says.

No, it probably wouldn't.

His arm squeezes me tighter to him. "I gotta go out of town Thursday. I might be back real late or not 'til Friday night. Not sure yet."

"Okay."

"Luck's gonna stay here and make sure you're protected."

I'm not sure how I feel about that. "Dante, I'm a little old for a baby sitter."

He chuckles softly. "Yeah. I know. Don't want you alone with Hemi still out there on the loose."

Huh. Well, at least now I know the club hasn't found and killed Logan.

"Okay."

His lips press against my forehead. "Good girl."

"Prom's Friday night. We get out at noon. I was going to get ready over at Athena's."

"Hmm...Wanted to see you before you left."

"You just saw me in my dress," I tease.

"And out of it."

We cuddle and joke around like that for a few minutes. Then Dante's hand smacks my ass. "Get some sleep. Got school tomorrow."

And I do as I'm told.

CHAPTER ELEVEN

KARINA

THERE'S a strange energy at school the next day. At first, I chalk it up to prom fever. Everyone's nervous and excited about the big night. A strange indifference surrounds me, but I'm not bothered by it. I've felt out of place among my classmates my entire life. Why should prom be any different? This disconnect between my classmates' concerns and mine has only grown over the years. Their fears and worries seem more childish than ever.

It used to be I couldn't wait to get out of this small town I've hated my entire life as soon as I graduated. I wanted to disappear in the middle of the night. See how long it took before my father or anyone else even knew I was missing. Now I'm torn. I don't know if I can be away from Dante for so long.

I also want to have a way to support myself. I love how he takes care of me, but it's frightening to think of being completely dependent on him. I've thought a lot about how he said time moves fast. And he's right. It seems like yesterday Athena and I came into this building as timid freshman.

Now we're bored seniors who can't wait to get the fuck out.

"Are you listening to me?" Athena asks, poking me with her plastic spork.

I brush whatever the hell she was eating off my shirt. "Ew, don't touch me with that thing."

"You want me to pick you up Friday morning, so we're not driving two cars?"

"Uh, sure. You don't mind driving all the way up there in the morning?"

"Nope."

I wonder what she'll think, if Luck's still at the house. I'll worry about it later.

"Okay. Then I can leave my dress in your car."

As we're leaving the cafeteria, the chatter around us increases in volume. "What's going on?" I yell into Athena's ear.

She shrugs. We duck around a group of jocks taking up way too much space and I almost smack right into Mr. Hackett. The gasp that shoots out of me draws his attention. We just stare at each other for a few seconds before he turns away.

"Wow," Athena whispers in my ear. "I heard someone say he got mugged or something last night."

Or something.

Something like Dante's fists.

Holy shit.

Did he really go beat Mr. Hackett up for what he said to me? The thought's terrifying. What if it makes Hackett come after me worse? What if Dante gets arrested and taken away from me?

I can barely concentrate on my schoolwork the rest of the day. As soon as classes are over, I ask Athena to drop me off at the clubhouse.

"I thought we were going shopping?" she whines.

"Please, it's important."

"Yeah, yeah."

She doesn't drive away when I get out, but I'm so focused on getting past one of the prospects, I can't worry about it.

"I'm Dante's girl," I tell him again.

"Don't matter. I'm not supposed to let anyone in."

"I don't think it applies to me."

I don't recognize this one. He runs his gaze over my body in a creepy way and shrugs. "Club girls are allowed in after three."

"I'm *not* a club girl," I spit out through gritted teeth. "Dante's your SAA, he's gonna be pissed if you don't let me in."

"Who the fuck you think told me not to let anyone in, bitch?"

That's it. Is Dante with another girl? Is that what this kid's trying to keep me from? Or is he really just that dumb? Either way, I whip out my phone and send Dante a text. Couple seconds later, Dante storms out and throws the kid against the wall.

"My woman tells you to let her in, you Let. Her. In."

Shit, I didn't even tell Dante the kid called me a bitch.

"Fuck, I didn't know! You said no one gets in—"

Dante cuts him off—by cutting off his air supply. His

fingers wrap tighter around the kid's throat. "Now you know."

He lets the kid go and holds his hand out to me. "What're you doing here, baby girl?"

I glance over at the prospect who's doubled over gasping for breath. I feel a little bad about it, but not much. I tried to warn him.

Taking my hand, Dante leads me inside. "I needed to talk to you."

One corner of his mouth twists up. "You needed to see me that bad?"

My cheeks heat up at the way he's staring at me. But I can't let myself get distracted by his sexy smile, rough voice, or lust-crazed eyes. There're people in the room, but they've all got Iron Bulls MC cuts on. Still, I lower my voice. "Did you beat up Mr. Hackett?"

Poof. Lust-crazed eyes and sexy smile disappear. "He bother you?" Dante's tugging me through the clubhouse so fast I can't answer.

"Dante, where are we going?"

"Need to show you something and I want to discuss this in private."

He leads me upstairs and opens one of the doors. This room is nice. Homey even. It has a giant bed similar to the one at home. Two dressers and even a vanity table. Best of all it has its own bathroom.

"What's this?"

"Our new room. I want you to be more comfortable when we gotta spend time here."

"You…you…did this for me?"

"Yeah." He shrugs. "Never gave a shit before."

My nose stings and my eyes water. Then I remember why I'm here. "Dante, Mr. Hackett. Is that what you had to do last night?"

His face hardens into something a lot sterner and a lot scarier.

"Don't ever question me about stuff like that, babe."

Dante

Fuck me. Never thought that uptight prick would actually go to work all beat to fuck. Figured he'd call in sick the rest of the week.

And Karina puttin' that together so quick. In the future, I gotta keep in mind how smart my girl is.

Her face falls from my harsh words. But she needs to understand something. Club business, my business, is not *her* business. Ever. I won't have any of my bad shit touchin' her.

Her bottom lip quivers and I almost apologize for bein' so sharp.

"Dante, you did that…for me? I can't even…what if?"

"What, babe? Spit it out."

She throws her body against me. Of course, I wrap my arms around her. She lets out a harsh sob. "I can't have anything happen to you. What if he talks to the police? I can't lose you."

Fuck me fucking sideways.

She ain't worried about what I did. She ain't worried about any blowback that might come her way. No, my little bitch is worried about *me.* Worried I might get taken away from her.

"Shh, baby girl. I'm fine. Nothin's gonna happen to me. He ain't talkin' to the cops—trust me. But you gotta understand something 'bout me, Karina. No one disrespects my girl. No one threatens you. There are consequences to fuckin' with what's mine."

"Dante," she sighs so sweet. "No one has ever made me feel…I've never…mattered to anyone—"

My mouth crashes into hers and we stumble over to the bed. My brain's on autopilot as I strip her down, and get my cock out. "You fuckin' matter to me, baby girl. I don't know how. Or why. But you matter more than anything," I growl against her throat as I shove inside her.

She whimpers and cries out. Her little hands furiously work to get my clothes off. Except I don't give her a second as I hammer into her. Finally, she gives up and hangs on to me.

"Dante," she whispers, and keeps whispering as I have my filthy way with her. There're words I want to give her but I can't just yet. They're in my head, but I don't know how to force them out. Instead, I keep giving her what I know how to give her. My dick and an orgasm or two. It's all I'm able to give right now, but I know it's not enough.

She deserves more.

CHAPTER TWELVE

DANTE

"You awake, baby girl?"

"No," she mumbles against my shoulder. "Died and gone to heaven," she adds with a soft giggle.

Well, isn't that enough to puff up my ego.

"Dante?"

"Yeah?"

"Thank you for…protecting me. Did you find out who—"

"Babe, what did I tell you?"

She gives me a blank look. Yeah, I said a lot of things before I pounded her into the mattress. "Don't question me about club stuff."

"But, it's not club stuff. It was about me. You could get in trouble because of me."

Fuck. How much am I gonna burden her with? "Luck was with me, so that makes it club stuff. You just forget about it, and go on like normal. He ain't gonna bother you again if he wants to live."

She hesitates and I see the dozen or so questions forming. Then she purses her lips, glances away and nods.

"Wanna go home?"

She sits up and brushes her hair off her sweaty forehead. "Can we? I love the room, Dante. Thank you—"

"But you're more comfortable at home?"

She nods.

"Get dressed."

I'm too mesmerized watching her naked ass wiggle back into her shorts to bother fixing myself up. Only when she throws me a questioning look do I finally get my ass in gear. This woman has the power to send every last one of my brain cells shooting out my dick.

And speaking of people who think with their dicks. When we get downstairs, Romeo's chatting up Karina's friend, Athena. Seems she never fuckin' left after droppin' my girl off.

Karina glances at me with worried eyes. As if I'm gonna be mad at her for my prez's bad judgment and her trouble-makin' little friend.

"Athena," she snaps, and then drags her out the front door.

"What the fuck you doin'?" I ask prez even though he's so focused on the front door, I doubt he heard me.

He turns to me with a filthy grin in place. "She's a fireball."

"She's a little young for you, don't ya think?"

Romeo laughs. "You fuckin' serious right now? She wouldn't have even been here if it wasn't for your cradle-robbing ass."

"Yeah, well, she's underage, so I'd wait on that one."

That finally wipes the smirk off his face. "She forgot to mention that."

"Yeah, I'm sure she did."

Karina comes through the door and hurries to my side. "I sent her home," she whispers.

Romeo lifts his chin at us. "Hey, Karina. You mind keepin' your jailbait friends outta my clubhouse?" He's laughing as he says it, but my girl's still upset. I drill him with a stare meant to shut him the fuck up.

"I'm sorry, Romeo. I didn't think she'd—"

"I'm just messin' with you. I'm the one who saw her waitin' outside and invited her in." He flicks his gaze at me and shrugs, then walks off. Karina doesn't seem to know what to do with that.

"Let's go home, baby girl."

At least I've given her a place to call home. I can do that much for her.

Karina

ATHENA WON'T SHUT up about Romeo. It's awkward when we're at her house tearing through her closet the next afternoon. While my father has barely ever been around, Athena's mom and dad give new meaning to the term "helicopter parent." They had Athena when they were older, so they've constantly worried and babied her. When we were younger, I was jealous of all the attention. Now, I'm grateful I don't have to put up with it. They'd drive me nuts. I have to give Athena credit though; our friendship is the one area she's always stood up to them about. They've never cared for their princess hanging out with a girl from the other side of town. I'm not sure if she's told them about my new living arrangements yet. Can't wait for that.

"You know if your mom overhears you, she's going to lock you in a closet," I whisper as she's showing me the earrings she got for prom night.

"I'm so outta here after graduation," she whispers back. "I've been saving every penny. I'm going to go to Los Angeles the day after my birthday.

"What? Since when?"

Her eyes take on a dreamy glaze. "Since forever."

"How come you never told me?"

She lifts her shoulders. "I figured you'd think it was stupid."

"Athena." Shit, I don't know what to say. How could my best friend hide something like that from me? "I'd never think that. I thought we were going to State together?"

"No. I'm going to try acting," she says with a straight face. What the hell? "I know what you're thinking."

I raise an eyebrow at her. "Do you?"

"I want to at least try. I won't be young and pretty forever."

I don't know how to respond to that.

We don't end up talking about it anymore.

When Athena drops me off, there's an unfamiliar bike in the driveway and I assume it means Luck reported for duty. I can't believe Dante basically asked his friend to babysit me. I'm mortified.

And touched that he cares about me so much.

Athena's in a hurry to get home and doesn't ask to come inside, thankfully. I'm not sure how I'd explain my bodyguard for the evening.

Dante's normally stone cold face warms when I walk in the door. I can't help flinging myself against him. As he wraps me up in his arms and slides his hands up and down my back, I'm finally able to shake off the uneasy feeling that followed me home from Athena's.

"Have fun with your girl?"

My shoulders lift. "I think she finally knows what she's wearing to prom."

He chuckles, and then turns me to face Luck, who's sitting on the couch watching us. "Hi, Luck," I greet softly while fluttering my hand in the air. Why am I so damn nervous? He's never been anything but nice to me. Well, he's also watched Dante get me off in the middle of the clubhouse once or twice. My cheeks warm from the memory.

"Hey, Karina."

"Do you have time to eat before you leave?" I ask Dante.

"No. I'm set. I'll try to be back before you leave in the morning."

"Okay." This is awkward, but I can already see Dante changing from the man I know at home, to whoever he becomes when he's wearing his Iron Bulls MC cut and out on club business. I get a final kiss on my forehead as he walks out the door.

Luck and I stare at each other.

"Got any homework?" he asks, then winces.

The awkward look on his face is enough to break the tension. For me anyway. I end up laughing, which makes him laugh too. "I'm sorry you got stuck babysitting me."

He rolls his lip and the corner of his mouth quirks into a smile. "I don't mind protecting you. Don't know what he'd do if Hemi came near you again."

My face warms even more. It's obvious to Dante's club brothers that I'm…important to him. The thought steals my breath.

"You okay?"

"Yeah, just hungry."

"I can make you—"

"No. I got it."

I end up making sandwiches for both of us. After some time, we relax in each other's company.

"Big night tomorrow?"

Did Dante really talk to his friend about my *prom*? "I guess."

"You don't seem excited."

Instead of answering, I get up and clear our dishes.

"Karina?"

Turning, I put my back to the counter, and cross my arms over my chest. "I'm not. It all seems very anticlimactic."

He snorts and a not unkind smile lifts his cheeks. "You're ready to move on. That's good. Some people never want to leave high school."

I hadn't thought of it like that. "I guess."

We end up watching Vampire Diaries together, which is weird, but fun. He doesn't crack any of the jokes I expected.

At ten, I let out a yawn and Luck glances at me. "You should probably head to bed."

I don't know what to say. It's sort of odd and bossy, but it doesn't bother me.

"Are you…are you, staying?"

"Yeah. I'll be down here. You're safe."

"Okay. Thank you."

It's strange going to bed without Dante here. Knowing someone else is in the house, I manage to fall asleep anyway.

Dante

"Christ, hurry up, you fuckers."

This job should *not* be takin' this long. Fuckin' prospects are slower than fuck. Or maybe I'm just antsy to get home and see my girl before she leaves for school.

One of the more corrupt gun dealers the club works with manages to "set aside" a large number of weapons every month. Then I get to help him transport them safely outside the state. It's dangerous, yet boring work. I *could* help the prospects unload the one van and load up the truck, but how will the little fucks learn if they never do the heavy lifting themselves?

I don't make it home until almost ten in the morning. Karina's gotta be in school, so I stop by the clubhouse first.

"How'd it go?" Romeo asks the minute I set foot inside.

"Fine. Long." I thrust the envelope of cash I was given at him and he takes it, counts it, and then hands me my share.

I'll hand out just enough to the prospects so they can eat for the week.

If it were up to Romeo, they'd get nothing.

"Seen Luck?"

By the perverted gleam in my president's eye, I have a feeling I know the answer to this question.

"I'm pretty sure he's taking a strap to Amy's ass, last I checked."

Fucking wonderful.

I knock on his fuckin' door anyway. The visual on the other side is straight out of a low-budget bondage video.

"What's up, brother. I'm busy."

I lift my chin at Amy, who, at the moment, is naked on top of a black leather bench on all fours. Ass facing the door, so I get a good view of everything. It's hard to miss the red ropes wrapped around her wrists and ankles keeping her tethered to the bench. "I can see that."

Amy tries to turn her head, I assume to say hello. The ball gag strapped to her face prevents much more than some gibberish. Even though, I catch the hint of a smile and an excited gleam in her eyes.

Luck turns and pops her on the ass with a long red suede flogger. "Eyes forward. Don't move again."

Not the first time I've walked in on a similar scene.

We step in the hallway, but Luck keeps the door cracked and positions himself to keep an eye on Amy.

"Everything go okay?"

He nods once. "Yeah. No problems. Her friend picked her up this morning, said she's going over there after school to get ready. But I assume you knew that."

"Yeah." I tilt my head in Amy's direction. "Kinda early for whips and chains, no?"

The twitch of his mouth and the rubbing of his thumb against the handle of the flogger tell me he's only going to tolerate my intrusion for so long.

"It's never too early." He pushes the door open. Amy's hot. No doubt. She's perfect. A little tiny for my big brute hands. But all I can think about is stringing up Karina the same way. Luck catches my eye, and for a second I swear brother knows exactly what's on my filthy mind.

"You want in? I can take the gag out."

Okay maybe not. "Nah."

Amy turns and mumbles something. Luck whacks her a little harder with the flogger. "Someone needs discipline."

"I think someone just likes being flogged," I say loud enough for Amy to hear. She wiggles her ass in response. I raise an eyebrow at Luck. "Have fun." I swear he's almost weary as he shuts the door.

Muffled moans and screams follow me down the hall.

CHAPTER THIRTEEN

KARINA

ALL AFTERNOON I PRIMPED, styled my hair, painted my nails, did my makeup—every last predictable girly thing I could think of—with Athena and a couple other girls from school hoping it would get me in the mood for prom.

It didn't.

I can't relate to any of the kids in my class. The hotel ballroom where the prom is being held is nice enough. No doubt, some committee is responsible for the silver-foil stars and white twinkle lights hanging from the ceiling. A couple years ago, I might have found it magical. Now I don't care. The only place I don't feel out of place is with Dante. When it's just us, at home together. Not at his clubhouse where I can be assured there will be at least one jailbait joke every night. Maybe I won't feel so strange in Dante's world after graduation. Well, Luck didn't make me feel weird. We had a pleasant morning. He hadn't heard from Dante, which disappointed me, but it was nice not to be alone.

"Please dance with me," Athena begs as she takes my hands and drags me onto the dance floor. We dance. Or rather, I dance, and she flails around like a Ritalin-laced Kermit the Frog. Her happy energy finally clears some of my fog and I actually have fun. A few boys in our class join us and I don't think much of it.

Until I spot Dante by the open door. As usual, he's wearing jeans, a tight Harley T-shirt, boots and his Iron Bulls cut. He's casually leaning against the wall ignoring the stares from my teachers and classmates. Everyone else is forgotten as I hurry over to him. We don't even speak. I just jump into his arms, and he catches me, kissing me breathless, and then setting me down.

"I had to see how pretty you were," he whispers into my hair.

"I'm so happy you're here." Seeing him is worth the dirty looks I'm getting from my History teacher.

"You didn't have to leave your friends. I was gonna wait for you."

"No. I'm more than ready to leave."

He stops and scrutinizes my face. "You sure?"

"Yes."

He takes another glance and his face twists with revulsion. "Okay, yeah. I understand why you wanna go."

Instead of leaving right away, he insists I run back in and say goodbye to Athena. She pouts, but when she sees Dante waiting, her mouth twists into a dirty grin. "Yeah, I don't blame you. You're such a lucky bitch."

I really am.

Dante

I feel like one warped motherfucker watching my girl run in to tell her friends she's leaving. Am I seriously at a high school prom to pick up my girlfriend? What the fuck's happened to me?

Any doubts are wiped away as she comes running back with a big smile on her beautiful face. Christ, I'm fucked.

Like an idiot, I didn't consider that she'd be in a dress and heels when I brought my bike. "You okay?" I ask.

"Yup. I just want to go home with you."

I hadn't actually planned on taking her home. But we stop there long enough for her to change. She skips back down the stairs in simple jeans and a sweatshirt. Her hair's a little blown from the ride, but otherwise still pinned and sprayed into place. Reaching out, I tuck a few wayward strands behind her ear. "You're beautiful."

Her eyes flutter shut and she leans into my hand. "Thank you."

If we don't get out of here, I'm going to have her naked and bent over the couch in the next few seconds. Normally, that's great, but I want to make her night special. Maybe I'm feelin' some guilt over taking her away from the "normal" things she should be experiencing at her age.

When we get to my bike, she eyes the saddlebags and compression pack strapped to the back, but doesn't ask any questions. Fuckin' love the way she trusts me.

I take her back to the state park we've been to before. This time it's too chilly for skinny-dippin'.

"Oh, Dante, it's so pretty here at night," she gasps as she hands me her helmet. Of course, she kicks off her shoes and runs for the water. "Not tonight, baby girl. Too cold."

She purses her lips into a playful pout and comes running back to me as I'm unstrapping the bags. "What's that?" she asks.

"Sleepin' bags."

"We're staying?"

"Yeah, isn't that supposed to be what prom's all about, staying out all night?"

Her wide eyes and parted lips stop me. That face fucks me up every fucking time. We find a good spot and I set everything down. She's still watching me as I roll out the sleeping bag. "Is that big enough for both of us?" she whispers.

"Yeah, babe." I've had about all I can take tonight. From picking her up in that so-fucking-modest-it-made-me-crazy dress to the fuck-me eyes she's giving me, I can't wait another second. "Take your shirt off."

Her mouth pulls up in a half-smile. "But you said it was too cold."

"Take. It. Off."

She's got some lacy, push-her-tits-up bra on and I tell her to leave it. Leaves crinkle under my feet as I move around and behind her. Other than her increased breathing, it's the only sound. I run my fingers down the smooth line of her neck, over her collarbone and down to cup her tits. Her hard-as-bullets nipples are begging for my fingers. I pull the fabric enough to expose her to the night air and she hisses, leaning back so her head's against my chest. She moans softly as I cup her tits in my hands, rolling her nipples between my fingers. "Did you miss me last night?" I whisper against her ear.

"Yes."

"Show me."

She struggles to turn, but I keep her in place. "Take your jeans down." She can't bend over, with me holding her like this, but she pushes them over her ass. I get a glimpse of juicy, round cheeks and pull away to take in her barely-there thong. My hands gently squeeze her tits to get her attention. "Who you wearin' all this sexy underwear for?"

"You."

My lips find her neck, kissing and sucking until she's squirming. "Touch yourself."

"What?"

"Slide your fingers down and touch your cunt."

She squeaks in surprise but does it. Too slow for my animal needs. I swat her hand away, and work two fingers inside her. "Like this, baby girl." Her eyes are closed and I doubt she heard me. She's too busy whimpering and bucking against my hand. I pull back to rub my wet fingers over her clit. "You like that, don't you."

"Yes. So much."

"Good girl." I keep playing her, fingers in her cunt, hand squeezing her tits until she comes on my hand. A soft, trembling orgasm. She sighs and keeps grinding into my hand. "Not enough, baby girl?"

"God, no. More."

My dick's begging for release and I can't deny it any longer. We tumble down onto the sleeping bag. My hands work her pants and sneakers off so fucking fast it isn't funny. But she's working my belt loose and shoving my pants down just as furiously. "You have any idea what you do to my fuckin' dick?"

"No. Show me."

Love the way my little bitch gets sassy when I'm about to fuck her. "Spread those legs wide and let me in." I'm lost as I force myself inside. "Take it."

"Give me." Love how she begs for my dick. Then we're just animals, grunting, thrusting, and pounding. Her hands grip my shoulders and slide down my arms. "Harder."

"I fuck you any harder, you're gonna be in the ground," I grunt even as I slam into her. Her hands leave my arms to grip my face, pulling me down for a kiss. I kiss her long, hard, and deep. We keep sucking and nipping at each, and it's like nothing I've ever experienced before. And I've experienced a lot.

I love her.

Fuck.

The burning want has nothing to do with how hot a fuck she is. I need her. All of her. A man like me. This girl. There's no going back from here. Not after her. No bitch would ever measure up.

We come together in a frantic, screaming rush.

"Baby girl, look at me." She opens her eyes, but I can't meet them. I kiss her forehead instead.

"I love you."

Karina

"Oh, my God."

And I burst into tears. Not just any tears, but breathless, ugly tears. It's too much. Too many years of loneliness and hurt. Underneath all that an all-consuming—

"I love you too," I whisper.

This is happening. We don't make sense.

Except we do.

"Why you cryin'?" he asks as he kisses my tears away.

Oh, my God. This man who is so restrained and downright frightening letting go. Telling me he loves me. "I don't know." The words come out garbled between hiccups.

"You love me though?"

Hic. "Yeah."

"Good."

I hook my legs around him and pull him closer. His lips find my forehead again. "Baby, I'm spent." He presses more kisses against my cheeks and over the tops of my breasts. Lazily pushing in and out of me as if he doesn't want to leave.

We still stay that way. Eventually, Dante moves us into the sleeping bag.

In the middle of the night, I wake up with my teeth chattering. "Dante," I whisper, trying to snuggle closer. Trying to crawl inside his warmth. "I'm cold."

"I'll warm you up," he rasps, entering me again. I'm sore from how rough we were before, but he goes at a sleepy pace until the warm glow of pleasure pulses through me. "Better?"

"Yes."

There's no frenzy this time. It's soft, sweet, and sleepy sex. He comes with a loud groan.

"Warmer?"

"Sort of."

"Let's go home."

We pack up and leave the park in the middle of the night. Just as we pull up to the house, the sun's starting to rise. "We should have stayed at the park," I whisper as we walk up the stairs.

"We'll do it again."

And I hope it's true.

CHAPTER FOURTEEN

DANTE

THE WORLD KEEPS RIGHT on spinning. I finally told my girl how I feel about her. She feels the same and that's that. I end up having to make another run and Luck gets stuck staying at my house. This time at least I'm home early. I find him half asleep stretched out on my couch.

"How's she doin?"

"Fine, went up to bed a while ago." He sits up and lifts his chin at me. "How was it?"

"Same old."

He runs his fingers through his hair until it's standing up. "Shit, she's sweet."

And I just *stare*.

"Sorry," he mumbles and looks away.

"It's fine. We hear anything about Hemi?"

That's a good topic.

"No. It's fuckin' bullshit how he can disappear into thin air. Unless someone's giving him shelter and lying to our fuckin' faces."

Yeah, I've been considering that angle myself.

"I'm thinking of taking a ride up to Bolt's."

Luck's eyebrow goes up. "I wouldn't go alone, brother. We got peace with the Savage Dragons right now, but who knows. Smallest thing could set that off."

"How's Amy's ass?" I ask, just to be a dick.

He snorts and looks away. "Fine. She's a good girl. But she's not the type of sub I'm looking for."

I must be dumber than fuck. It takes a second to get what he's trying to say. Then it makes sense why the fuck he was flogging the shit out of Amy hours after spending the night here.

With *my* girl.

"Karina is?" I ask quietly. It's not much of a question. I already know the answer.

"No, brother."

He's got enough respect for me to lie. It's weird, but I'm not pissed. Anyone else hinted at that shit would be getting the ever-loving fuck kicked out of him right now.

"We'll talk about it another time. I'm fuckin' beat. You can stay if you want."

"Nah, I'll head out."

My girl's sound asleep when I make it upstairs. Curled up on her side. Just the barest glimpse of her ass in the dull moonlight gets my dick hard. Or maybe it's knowing my brother's lusting after my girl.

Doesn't matter. She's gettin' woken up either way.

Karina

Dante slides into bed. And even though I don't think he meant to, the motion wakes me. He rolls over sliding his hand under my shirt and over my hip. My body shies away. "Why ain't you sleepin' naked?" he rasps against my shoulder.

I turn more and pull my knees up to my chest. "Can't."

His big hand slides to my back, rubbing and kneading. Oh, why is he torturing me like this? A shiver of delight hardens my nipples. As if he's in tune with my body, he reaches over and cups my breast, rolling and teasing my nipple until I moan.

"Dante, stop."

"No. Want my girl. Come here."

"I can't."

He hooks his arm around my waist and yanks me to him. Oh God, the hard, hot length of him is poking into my back. *I want.* My pussy throbs with need.

"Why?" he demands.

"It's my time of the month," I whisper, completely mortified.

His body shakes against mine, and he slides my hair off my shoulder. Soft lips kiss and lick at my neck. "Baby, I don't give a fuck," he whispers in my ear.

My body shudders from the raw desire in his voice. "Real men ain't scared of gettin' a little war paint on their dicks," he says.

"Dante?"

He slides his hands under my tank and urges me to sit up so he can take it off. Gently, he brushes his hands over the hard tips of my nipples. A soft moan leaves my throat and he growls against my back. "They sore, baby girl?"

"No," I whisper.

"Want me to suck on 'em?"

God yes. But I remain quiet. I don't want to get any more turned on than I already am. Getting excited only makes my cramping worse. I don't know what the hell he meant by war paint on his dick, and I'm too afraid to find out.

His lips press against my shoulder, traveling down until he flicks his tongue over one nipple and then the other.

"Could suck on these like candy all night," he whispers against my skin. He keeps licking, nipping and sucking, until I'm panting and squirming under him.

"Baby girl wants my dick."

"No," I moan, even as my hand slides down his stomach, brushing against the hard length of him.

"Yeah, you do." The bed rolls as he gets out. He comes out of the bathroom naked, hard cock leading the way, and a stack of towels in his hands. "I got towels and a shower, baby girl, so I'm gettin' in that pussy. You got fifteen seconds to do whatever you gotta do and get back here ready to be fucked."

His words scare and excite me at the same time. I throw back the covers and race into the bathroom. When I return he's standing by the side of the bed stroking his cock. I hesitate by the bathroom door and we stare at each other from across the room.

"You're fuckin' gorgeous, baby girl. Look like a fuckin' angel with all that light behind you." My heart kicks up at his words. "Come here."

Slowly, I make my way over. When I'm within arm's reach, he yanks me to him. I gasp from the sudden rush of arousal pouring through me. He twists his hand into my hair, holding me for a deep kiss. A soft whimpering sound leaves me as he works me into a needy frenzy. Big hands gather my hair in a makeshift ponytail and he tugs.

"Knees."

I realize there's s folded towel on the floor and I drop to it.

"Suck."

Thank god. Maybe this is all he wants and I happily wrap my mouth around his cock, moaning at how good he tastes. He hisses in a jagged breath when I take him all the way to the back of my throat, then uses my hair to pull me off him.

"What?" I ask.

"Get up on the bed."

"Dante, no. I'm all gross."

His hand tightens in my hair. "Nothin' gross about you."

"I'm all crampy."

"An orgasm or two will help."

Thinking he's kidding, I snort.

"It's Dante recommended." His low voice makes my insides shiver. "Better than any Advil. Now, I want that pussy. Get. On. The. Bed."

Dear lord, when he uses that tone, there's not a molecule in my body that wants to resist.

He's laid towels on the bed and I gingerly sit on the edge. He climbs on and pulls me down with him. One of his arms draws me close and his other hand kneads and plays with my breasts. "So, fucking perfect," he whispers, dipping his head to suck and tease each nipple until I'm moaning and writhing.

"That's my girl. Missed you," he murmurs against my lips, rolling me under him. His big, warm, rough body covers mine and a thrill runs through me. It's dirty and wrong. But he's got me wanting it so bad now, I don't even care. His cock rubs up against my pussy, and he groans. "It's gonna feel so good, baby. You're all slick for me."

My cheeks heat up and I roll my eyes, making him chuckle. My laughter turns into a gasp as he pushes inside me in one, long, slow thrust.

"Oh, oh, Dante. That's…that—"

"Feels good, baby girl?"

"Yes," I sob as he thrusts into me a little deeper.

"You want more?"

I shake my head. I can't say it. It feels obscene and nasty, but so fucking good. "I feel so dirty," I whisper.

He chuckles and kisses my forehead. "Baby, I'm the filthiest fucker you'll ever meet. You're my dirty little girl. I love fuckin' you any way I can get you. Don't ever say no to me because you're embarrassed. Got nothing to hide from me." He growls the last part against my neck.

I can't answer, because he adjusts the angle of his hips and each time he slides into me, he brushes against my clit. "Oh, fuck. Dante, right there."

He rolls us so I'm on top. "Wanna watch you ride me, dirty girl. Get me filthy." I've lost the ability to think or form any thoughts other than *up, down, grind, harder, more*. "Fuck. Oh, fuck. Dante."

"Come for me. You feel so good, dirty girl. So fuckin' warm and tight and slick. Come all over my cock for me." Tingles of heat travel from my breasts, where he's caressing and pinching the stiff tips. My orgasm pushes against me, pressure inside, trying to find a way out.

"I can't," I pant out breathless and frustrated. Dante's hand cups my chin, forcing me to look at him.

"Yeah, you can. I'm right here. We got all night. Relax." His hands cup my hips, urging me up and down. "Ride my dick."

"Fuck!" The tension breaks, swift and hard enough to bow my back until I feel the ends of my hair tickling Dante's thighs.

"That's it, dirty girl. Don't stop." I keep moving. Couldn't stop even if I wanted to and my orgasm continues. "Ah, ah, ah," I gasp. And it hurts, but in the best way.

I fall down over him and he chuckles against my hair, running his hands up and down my back, squeezing my ass, while pumping up into me. "Can you take me, baby girl?" he asks with a sexy growl. "Can you take more of my cock?"

"Yes." I can do anything if this feeling lasts.

He hammers up, hard and fast, gripping and squeezing my ass. His jaw drops and he throws his head back, jerking into me with a deep groan. I feel closer to him than any one in my entire life.

His eyes open and he smiles at me. I think I'm the only one he smiles for like that. "Kiss me, baby girl." I shift and from the liquid squish of things, I can only imagine the mess we've made. As if he's reading my mind, he puts his hand at the back of my head and takes his kiss. He rolls us again, pinning me underneath him. Staring down at me, he kisses my cheeks and forehead.

"You good?" he asks.

I nod. "So good." I'm still tingly all over.

He places one hand over my belly. "Still hurt?"

"No," I answer before realizing it's true.

"Let's get cleaned up. Wait here."

I close my eyes, because I don't even want to know. But I can hear him run through the room and start up the shower, then return for me. "Okay, dirty girl. Time to get clean." He chuckles and scoops me up.

The loving way he soaps me up in the shower is a complete contrast to the dirty way he just fucked me in the bedroom.

When we're clean and back in bed, he pulls me tight to his chest. "Need you to meet me at Romeo's tomorrow. I got a car for you to look at."

"Okay. Thank you."

This man makes my head spin.

CHAPTER FIFTEEN

DANTE

ROMEO ASKED me to come help him work on a few cars this afternoon. Since I'm not in the habit of saying no to my president, and I plan to meet Karina here, that's where I spend my day. The car he got for her is perfect. Newer than the last one. I also put a tracker in that shit. Ain't risking losing my girl again.

Three o'clock my dick's hard, like it knows she's about to show up.

What do you know? Two minutes later, Athena's car pulls into the parking lot. Romeo, moron that he is, swaggers out to meet her. Karina gives me an uninhibited kiss right there in front of everyone and I'm a happy fuck.

Two seconds later, I'm a homicidal fucker.

"Tucker, what's up?" Romeo shouts to Karina's father.

Karina's big blue eyes blink up at me. "Tucker?" Her gaze strays to her father and the two of them stare at each other. Then his eyes shoot to the possessive way I'm holding onto his daughter.

Go on motherfucker. Test me.

The way he's neglected his daughter. The pain he's caused her. I'm ready to put a bullet in his head right now. Him staring at us like that is handing me the perfect excuse.

"Karina?" He nods at me. "Dante?"

"You know each other?" she asks me.

"Yeah, I've known Tucker a while now. How you been?" I ask real casual to see how he wants this to go down.

Tucker's gaze shoots to Romeo then back to Karina.

"What're you two doing together?"

"Um, Dante and I are together. It's his house I moved into. I tried calling you."

Tucker's guilty gaze swings back to Romeo who finally has something to say. "Yeah, motherfucker. Looks like you owe me a daughter."

Karina

"Looks like you owe me a daughter."

What the hell? My head's spinning. My dad knows Dante and Romeo. So Logan wasn't lying after all.

"Since this one's with my Sergeant-at-arms," Romeo continues, "looks like it's gonna be the other one."

Other one?

"I don't have any sisters," I say.

Dante's arm tightens around my shoulders. Romeo glances at me, then back at my father. His mouth curls into a fierce smile. He shakes his head. "Tucker, you been keepin' big family secrets?"

"Dad? What's he talking about? I don't have a sister."

And I still haven't forgotten that whole "owe him a daughter" comment.

"Karina, I was going to explain—"

"Explain what? What's he talking about?"

"I—"

"He's got a whole 'nother family up north," Romeo finishes for my dad.

"Is that true?"

My father finally looks me in the eye. "Yes."

Dante and Karina's story continues in
Entwined (Iron Bulls MC #3)

ALSO BY PHOENYX SLAUGHTER

Asunder (Iron Bulls MC #1)

Disconnect (Iron Bulls MC #2)

Entwined (Iron Bulls MC #3)

Vexed (Iron Bulls MC #4)

Unhinged (Iron Bulls MC #5)

Dirty Side Down (Iron Bulls MC Boxed Set #1)

Infatuation

IRON BULLS MC
PHOENYX SLAUGHTER

www.ingramcontent.com/pod-product-compliance
Lightning Source LLC
Chambersburg PA
CBHW061242170626
46809CB00007B/2782

* 9 7 8 1 9 4 3 9 5 0 8 2 9 *